BOOK ELEVEN OF THE RIM CONFEDERACY

Honeymoon Bottle

by Jim Rudnick

RUDNICK PRESS

ISBN-13: 978-1-988144-23-8
Copyright © 2016
Jim Rudnick

 RUDNICK PRESS

For my Susan...

Dear Reader...

Thank you for reading this ebook.

If you have borrowed this book through the Kindle Unlimited subscription program, I kindly ask that —

— **you click through to the last page of this book when you are finished reading and exit the book!**

This will ensure that the author is properly credited for the book borrow...

Thank you...

Jim Rudnick

The RIM Confederacy:
Honeymoon Bottle

"Recovering from almost fatal wounds at the hands of his sister, Tanner finds the time spent on the beach on Bottle a great way to recharge and think about his future too. Finding a way to save his sister is one major item on his plate but then there is the late Duke's Will and the codicil offer that was beyond his wildest expectations—what to do?

The Barony had other issues, from the new discovery of more ancient relics on the crashed alien ship on Ghayth to the news that the Baroness was out once again, trying to expand her realm. When a mysterious package arrives sent to the Ambassador in charge of the Duchy, the secret is out and the hunt for a new Duke is now public news.

As the RIM Confederacy Council meeting convenes to decide the fate of the Duchy of Neen, the whole Confederacy is surprised and Provost Guards enter the room to keep the peace—which may or may not last past the end of the meeting, never mind lasting for the whole RIM Confederacy!"

A Message to you from the Author...

I just wanted to say thanks so so much for reading Book Eleven of the RIM Confederacy!

As my Amazon bio says, being a youngster in the 1950's meant that I was a voracious reader in what has been called the Golden Age of Science Fiction. That meant that for me, my heroes were not on the hockey rink or gridiron - but instead in my local Library where at 12 I had a full Adult card (thanks Dad!) and took out more than 5 books a week.

Everyone from Heinlein, Norton, Leiber, Pohl, Anderson, Simak, Asimov, Brackett, Gunn, Van Vogt and more....I fell in love with and eventually owned Ace Doubles of my own. And while I never knew who wrote the Tom Corbett - Space Cadet series, I fell in love with them and they had a place of honor on my own bookcase too!

With that kind of an introduction to Science Fiction, it's no wonder that when I got my writing work done, I turned my own fictional side of my brain to writing same. It's one thing I know how to write - and a totally different matter to release same to the world - something that I've just started to work on....

Suffice it to say my own works are rooted in that Golden Age and it's that era that I'd like to one day be known as a teensy contributor to in some small way...

So once again, thanks for beginning my RIM Confederacy series and wait'll you learn about the alcoholic spaceship captain that is my hero, who fights and beats aliens but not the bottle!

Enjoy and remember, in a series, characters develop and mature not the way we sometimes want...instead, it's like they have a life of their own!

And while you can read the series in any order, I'd highly recommend to start with Pirates, then Sleeper Ship, Prison Planet, Ancient Relics, Hospital Ship, Desert Planet, Ruined Memories, Eons Semester, Trade Wars, Brothers Pride and Honeymoon Bottle too...and yes, there's more coming soon too!

Prologue ~

He rolled to his left, leaned up on his elbow, and looked as usual to the horizon. The blue of the ocean faded right into the blue of the sky, and he was in paradise. Beside him, slowly adding more color to her already deep tan, his bride lay dozing in the bright Bottle sun.

Every day was like the one before. Each day started with a clear blue sky and an early morning breeze that took the heat off one's body, and by late afternoon, there were always some clouds and the heat mellowed out as the occasional cloud obscured the sun.

Since they owned the resort, their requests were promptly met. All Tanner had to do was clear his throat, and their casita AI would immediately call a steward who'd trot out to the edge of the pool to take a drink order. Or a snack order. Or an order for just about anything he could ask for.

He'd jokingly asked Helena once if he could order the steward to kill the cook as he'd not really liked a dish—and immediately he'd turned white and had choked back his grief. Having lost a friend like the Duke d'Avigdor just a month ago and the Master Adept as well, he realized his attempt at humor was not something that he countenanced at all. Helena had cuddled him, smiled at him, and calmed him, and they'd gone back to tanning in the sun. The funeral for David, the Duke D'Avigdor, had been one of the hardest things he'd ever had to do, and he was thankful he'd had such great support.

On Bottle, at their resort, all he had to do was to recuperate. His chest still showed the scars of the gunshot wound and the robo-doc surgery that had saved his life. As brand new scars often do not tan so well, his chest looked odd, he thought. His physiotherapist, who still came to see him every other day to assist him with the exercises that were supposed to help, told him that was to be expected.

Tanner thought the exercises did help a bit, as he leaned on his left elbow and stretched a little to test the newly grown sternum and its musculature. No pain anymore, which was good. Maybe it was time to have physio say only once a week, he thought.

He lay back down, and closing his eyes, he wondered for the millionth time today what Gia was doing.

She was still being held on Neres in the same jail he'd been kept in a few years back. She had no rights as a citizen of the RIM Confederacy, as she was obviously guilty of killing two people—the Issian Master Adept and the Duke d'Avigdor—both his friends. He wondered what she thought she was doing when she'd come to his wedding to kill him. Why she couldn't accept that he had not killed their sister Nora—not even by accident as the Branton Tribunal had found him innocent—was something he didn't understand.

He thought about what he was going to do with her. When he and his bride had left for their somewhat delayed honeymoon on Bottle, the Baroness had told him she would hold Gia until he returned and he would decide her fate.

He rubbed his chest, felt the still rough scar edges, and wondered what Gia's fate might be …

CHAPTER ONE

The Baroness lay half-reclined on her loveseat and toyed with Gracie, her pet cat. At least she called it a cat. It had four legs and a sort of feline face, which was enough for her. The fact that it walked sideways crossing one leg over the other to move was not worth even thinking about. "A cat is a cat," she said to herself as she stroked its back just above its two tails. Of course, cats purred, but Gracie was mute as she stretched up to get the maximum itching from her master. The Baroness sighed and reached over with the other hand to the table at her side.

The wine was gone, she saw and thought about calling for more, but then she stopped.

The ambassador of the Duchy d'Avigdor was due in just a few more minutes, and she had her issues with how she wanted to play the man.

With six planets in the realm, the duchy was small but still a very worthy prize. At ten planets, her Barony was now the second largest realm in the RIM Confederacy and she was always looking to expand. One day, she was sure, the Barony would be the biggest realm in the Confederacy, and she couldn't wait forever for that to occur.

The leader of the duchy, David the duke d'Avigdor, had been killed during her stepdaughter's wedding just a month ago, and the duchy was without a leader. A pro-tem provisional government along with guidance of the Executive Council of the Confederation was now running the duchy d'Avigdor.. The combined group was charged with the duty to preserve the duchy but at the same time to plan its own future without a hereditary successor as the next duke.

She grinned and said, "More wine. Same as last time, please," and the sitting room AI chimed back that her order had been heard and acted on.

In less than a minute, an EliteGuard appeared from a side door and quickly removed the empty glass and replaced it with a full one.

Red. She was drinking red for a change, from the best Quaran burgundy vintages they had. Her wine sommelier had offered that it was fine to drink now —it was already aged five years in Anulet oak—but if she chose to buy some to lay down in the cellars, she would be able to drink the very enhanced vintage for at least another twenty years. That had interested her somewhat as she normally drank light whites and their age was not so important she knew.

She'd ordered a hundred cases and had even gone down the two elevators and the escalator to the sub-basement floor to see them in the cellar. With more than thirty thousand bottles, the Barony cellars were something to see, she had thought. First created by her husband years before he'd even met her, his love of Quaran wine so great that the size, depth, and breadth of the cellars was well known all across the RIM. She had added little, but as she walked the aisles between the racks of bottles, she knew she'd never get to drink all or even a healthy percentage of the wealth of wines around her. She'd instructed her sommelier to present her with a new red each week for her to taste and try. Last week's wine had been just too, too much like tasting sweaty socks for her to enjoy at all, and she'd commented about that. The sommelier had nodded and had said this kind of wine, a Côtes du Rhône clone, was often associated with that typical smell and taste—too much yeast was the reason he said. She remembered nodding, as if she understood that, but she had added never again, please to that offering.

Today, the red was from a grape she'd never tasted before—at least that's what the sommelier had said. The Nebbiolo grape, he had said, was the king of grapes. This wine had been aged for more than ten years in Anulet oak, using old often-used casks that imparted slow, slow oaky tastes to the vintage. She sipped it once more and smiled.

"Truly a king," she said to herself, "just like I should be," and that got a real out loud laugh.

The side door opened up once more and an EliteGuard came over to her. "Ma'am, the ambassador of d'Avigdor is without. Should I let him in?"

She sat up and Gracie moved over to take the far end of the loveseat as she rose to straighten her appearance and tidy her hair. That took her almost two minutes, and then she nodded to the guard who left the room to return with the ambassador.

Humans tend to all look the same, she thought, and when they have a diplomatic rank like an ambassador, they are very particular about their appearance. The man was just over six feet tall with wavy white hair, and his face was handsome in a mature way. His blue eyes were focused on her as he walked the distance from the far door to stand before her.

He half-bowed, as she was Royalty, and he smiled as he held out his hand to her. "So nice for you to be able to see me, Ma'am. The duchy thanks you for the opportunity to speak to you," he said.

She nodded back, clasped his hand for a second, and then turned to retake her place on the loveseat. Across from her on the other loveseat, the ambassador sat and leaned forward toward her.

When she reached for her wine, she saw he did not have anything. Trying to be hospitable was one way of winning over a diplomat. "I was just trying this new wine, would you care to join me with a small glass, Ambassador?" she inquired.

He hesitated, and she watched the indecision flicker over his face as he contemplated accepting a drink even though it wasn't noon. He nodded and said, "Yes please, Baroness, I'd love to try it too," and he smiled.

She nodded and moments later, the EliteGuard presented him with a glass of the wine too.

She held out her glass and toasted to him. He followed suit, swirling the vintage in his glass a couple of times as he took a big sniff of the bouquet, and then he took a good-sized sip followed. He sucked in a bit of air then too, aerating the vintage in his mouth, and then swallowed it, savoring the mouth feel and the long-lasting finish too.

His eyebrows shot up. "Ma'am, I have never ever

tasted anything so … so … so regal. This is a Nebbiolo, Ma'am, but so much better than anything I'd ever had the opportunity to try. Thank you so very much," he said as he took another sip too and then set the glass down.

She nodded and made a mental note to gift the man with some of same, and then she smiled at him.

"So glad you like it, Ambassador," she said.

She did not offer up anything else as she was playing a wait and see game with him that she often did with people who came to her looking for something. She had no idea what it was that the man—or the duchy—wanted. She wanted him to take the lead.

He smiled at her and leaned back.

"Ma'am, I come to you today to make an offer— directly from our own Duchy Provisional Government about the future of the duchy. As you well know, Ma'am, the duke had no heirs. No natural-born child to inherit the dukedom—which puts our realm in somewhat of a predicament," he said. His voice was polished, and he had the oration skills that came with decades of diplomatic talks.

He knew where he was going, she thought, which meant that the Duchy had plans …

"So we would like to talk to some other realms— other meaning the few that we think would be a

16

great candidate for us to, well, the word merge comes to mind. We would like to be a full partner with an existing RIM Confederacy realm, and the Barony is one of our candidates," he said and smiled at her once more.

We would love to own the duchy. She smiled back.

"We would certainly love to begin those talks, Ambassador. Might I ask how many candidates there are that you have under consideration?" she said sweetly, sipping from her glass and showing her enjoyment of the wine to him. Nothing better than reminding him of what was in his glass too, she thought.

He looked away and then back at her. "Ma'am, that is not something that I'm allowed to mention, but I can tell you that the list is very, very short. In fact, we've already been approached by almost a dozen other interested parties too. But we're using our own list and vetting each of the candidates, Ma'am," he said.

She nodded. As she'd thought, RIM Confederacy realms were all interested, but most were much smaller than the duchy. There were only a couple bigger or about the same size, and the Barony alone lay right on their borders too as the closest candidate. That was a good sign, she thought.

"Then please, have your team get in touch with

my own and we can at least begin talks, Ambassador," she said.

He nodded and reached for his glass one more time. He sipped the last of the wine and smiled again.

After he'd left, the Baroness sat and contemplated this new issue. While she had to admit the Duchy d'Avigdor was well worth the effort as a prize, she did have some misgivings about the other candidates.

I need to find out who else is on that list and what I might be able to do to erase them as competitors—not a real problem, she thought. Not hardly at all …

#####

He rolled to his left and tucked the single top sheet between his legs. For the tenth time, he tried to fall asleep. He lifted his head to glance over at Helena, who was snoring lightly on his left. He watched her chest rise and fall with each breath, and he wished he too were asleep. He laid his head back down on the pillow and turned a bit so he could see the ceiling of the casita and its layered roof of reeds in the slight glow from the ocean just outside. Somewhere up there was that green gecko that he'd spied often over the past couple of months spent here on Bottle.

"Some honeymoon," he said to himself. "Me, my bride, and my gecko." Not that the lizard was a bad casita roommate. Sometimes, he chirped a few times or even in a long string of chirps that made him feel like he was the trespasser here. No matter, as usual at night, the gecko was hunting prey to eat, and against the dark brown reed ceiling, he couldn't see the greenish lizard at all.

He rolled a bit farther back to stare straight up at the ceiling.

Sleep didn't come with his mind a mesh of ideas and complications and issues he had to get ahold of, but after two months on Bottle, he knew that what he needed to do first was to go home. Back to Neres and the Barony Palace to work out what his new duties as Lord Scott might be.

"Too many issues to think on," he said to himself, and for some reason the duke—his best man at his wedding—jumped into his consciousness.

He had so very much liked the man. As a mentor, the duke d'Avigdor had been very helpful to Tanner when he'd arrived here on the RIM only a decade or so ago. He had credited the duke with saving his life when he'd been ambushed by a Jael, the huge predator that lived on Anulet. The duke had blasted him from the rear as the Jael had been standing over him, and the Jael had died, which had saved Tanner's life. But then the Jael's mate

19

had showed up, and he'd been the one to shoot that snarling beast, and the duke's life had been saved. By him. Each had saved the other, and the two dead Jaels had paid the price.

He'd been injured with a broken leg, and time in the robo-doc had been needed to fix that injury. The Duke had thrown a huge planet-wide party in honor of him for saving his life, which had been more than enough. It had really not been a planned thing—getting ambushed on a hunting planet by the trophy that you're looking for had been one thing—and both he and the duke had escaped with their lives.

He shook his head slightly, and a few drops of sweat came off his brow and dripped on the pillow. He rolled all the way over onto his right hip and crawled to the edge of the bed to find cooler sheets to lie on. He smiled to himself.

The duke had said something to him at his bachelor party—that he had a special honor for Tanner and he'd find out after the wedding. Gia, his sister, had shot and killed the duke at the altar on his wedding day, and Tanner had not found out what that honor was—until the duke's funeral.

Heads of state and their funerals, he'd not known, were a very big thing out here on the RIM. Every single Confederacy member and all of their realm planets sent representatives—heads of state themselves in most instances. He'd been just out of the robo-doc after being shot at his wedding, and he'd insisted on going to Neen, the home planet of the Duchy d'Avigdor, to attend the funeral. His new wife and her stepmother, the Baroness, had insisted on sending along a full medical team too, which was a pain, but they'd all gone to Neen to attend the event.

He wiped his brow. Sweaty still. He cleared his throat and said to the casita AI, "Breeze on me, please, say, fifteen mph."

From somewhere, a nice breeze hit his face and body. Evaporative cooling, he thought, as the breeze began to chill him as the sweat began to evaporate. "If I had to invent something science-wise," he said to himself, "it'd be just that. Cool off in the breeze …" He pushed back the remembered prognosis from his doctor that he might have some issues with not being able to sleep or going over the event time and time again. He could force off the event memory, but sleep seemed to be beyond him frequently.

He snorted and brought his mind back to the duke's funeral, leaving his contributions to science out of his consciousness.

The duke d'Avigdor's funeral was held at the duke's palace and had taken place in a wing that had been used for ducal funerals for many generations. There had been no casket as the duke had been cremated. His ashes had been bottled up and sent via probe directly into the system's sun. According to tradition, all dukes were sent to the Neen system sun so they would always shine down on Neen.

He had not been out of the robo-doc for long, and he'd not really been able to pay attention to much before the ceremony, but he did appreciate that as a "new" Royal, he got to sit right up front with the Baroness and his wife. Around him were heads of state for many of the RIM realms, and he nodded to some he knew and smiled at Kondo, newly made the prime minister of Amasis, and also to his friend Bram, who came up to say hello and shake his hand. His friends were there and that made him feel a bit better, he remembered.

"Up by five more mph," he said, and the breeze got a bit stiffer and the cooling increased too.

He sat up, moved his legs off the bed, and slowly walked over to the bathroom in the far corner of the casita.

He sat on the toilet, rested, and wondered how the casita AI knew he had moved and kept the breeze constant. He looked around at the big shower stall, at the bidet beside him, and at the vanity off to one side. As an owner, he'd thought that the settings here in the southern ocean were what one might have called tropical rustic until one remembered that it was completely technologically supported.

There were force fields out in the water that protected the whole group of islands from just about anything and everything that Bottle could throw at them from typhoons to sharks. The waters around them were pristine with small, non-dangerous fish only. Each of the casitas looked handmade by someone hundreds of years ago, yet the resort was not even a year old yet. Beneath the larger of the islands, just a few hundred yards away, lay landing ports for ships and spaceships. His personal pilot, Lieutenant Cooper, had set down the *Sword*—his own personal ship—when they'd arrived here on Bottle those couple of months back. The *Sword* was a one-hundred-foot-long ex-personnel shuttle, which he'd had completely refurbished to make into his own ship in the Barony shipyard. He'd added very sumptuous quarters for himself and serviceable ones for crew too. Not that he needed much crew. Cooper was his helmsman, and he'd wanted Hartford too, but he had realized that this Barony officer belonged in the navy, and so he'd not taken him on. He had considered others too; as a Royal, he'd just command and the Barony Navy would comply, but he also knew that sometimes some personnel belonged where they'd be best for the Barony and not his own little world.

He sighed and stood. He hadn't had to go, but the seat had been cool at least. He trotted back to bed.

Back in bed, his thoughts wandered again to the duke's funeral. The funeral, he'd realized, had been long, but it didn't seem so at the time. Some speakers he'd not known had talked about the duke when he'd been a youngster—his own nanny had been one of them, he remembered. The chairman of the RIM Confederacy, Chairman Grasci, spoke too as had a few other heads of state. The brand new Master Adept had also spoken and had been more than supportive seeing as her predecessor had also been killed at the wedding.

He remembered wondering about that, as he shifted his arm under his pillow, bunching it up so his head would be a bit higher.

Wouldn't the Issians, who were mind readers and could sometimes "tell" what the future held, have known about the assassin and the plot to kill him? And if they knew, why did they not interfere —losing their own Master Adept?

He shook his head once more and noted that there was no sweat coming off his brow, which was a good thing.

Why indeed? He asked himself about that every

day. And he had no answer at all.

He had left the funeral, as he remembered, feeling very tired after sitting up for almost a whole afternoon. Robo-docs worked well, but the fatigue he felt was right through to the bone. He was glad for the arm of the nurse who helped him move from the pew to the chair, and then he was on his way back to the *Atlas* to go back to Bottle.

He'd paid his respects. He had very much liked the duke. Saying goodbye was hard in his condition, but he was glad he'd done just that.

As the group moved, led by the Baroness and her retinue, he was wheeled along near the rear of the whole Barony party, and at the doorway of the exit point, a single man stood, his eyes on Tanner. As he was slowly pushed toward the man, Tanner could see he was dressed as a member of the Duchy Diplomatic Corps with a green sash across his chest. He stepped forward and spoke quietly to Tanner while walking along at his side.

"Lord Scott, the duke has some private papers that were reserved for YOUR EYES ONLY. Might I suggest, My Lord, that when you're able to come back that you just let us know and we will arrange for you to get same?" he said as he straightened and turned on his heel to move back and away.

"Honey, you okay?" Helena said as she walked back to see the diplomat veer off. She snapped her fingers, and three EliteGuards appeared at her shoulder.

"Not a problem, dear." He waved off the guards. "He just thanked me for coming is all ..." he said, and they progressed out toward the *Atlas* to go back to Neres.

He wiggled his arm about a bit under the pillow, trying to find a spot where it was better, and he realized that he'd sort of lied to his wife—and he had no idea why. He wondered if other brand new husbands lied to their wives just days after the wedding, and he had no answer to that one. Nor, for that matter, did he believe that swearing to never lie to her again would be something he would be able to honor either. And as far as those ducal papers, they could wait.

"So much for being a husband ..." he said as his comfort grew and the cool air worked at slowly putting him to sleep.

#####

She really had not spent much time on Dessau itself, choosing always to fly in and then take a robo-cab up to the walled Issian city to see the Master Adept. But now as she was the new Master Adept, it had been somewhat forcefully mentioned to her that she should be prepared to visit the capital city, Dessau, at least once a month.

To walk among her citizens and to listen to them. To provide quiet counsel and offer up her advice as she faced their own issues, and to let them know that as their Master Adept, she cared for them all.

She had considered that as one of the job duties that came along with being the Master, and she would have to get used to them all. She had almost grinned, when she'd wondered about what else her aides would roll out on her for more duties to consider, and then she'd stopped short. She didn't know. How could one be a mind reader and see into the future and not know?

She had no idea. "What I do know was that I have much yet to learn," she said to herself as her aide opened the door for her on the robo-cab, and she stepped out in the downtown core of Dessau.

A city of more than 400,000 souls, it was a city under climate siege. The weather on Eons had turned bad more than a generation ago with constant droughts and higher than normal solar radiation placing their whole farming community in jeopardy. Without food, one starved. Or, one bought from off world, which was what Eons had been doing now for almost three hundred years. Generating the revenues to use to buy that food, she well knew, was hard as well. Thank God, the RIM Confederacy Naval Academy had been founded here, and all of those revenues were used just to feed Eons populations.

She looked over to her left first to see that some of the citizens were staring at her, stopped dead in their tracks at the sight of the planet's Master Adept. She nodded to them and then looked to her right as her aide pointed that way, and she began to walk along beside her. Ahead a group of youngsters had also frozen, their mouths open.

She smiled at them, and when she was about in the center of the dozen young girls and boys, she stopped and turned to face them. "Hello," she said and she waited, her mind reaching out to look among the brains in front of her.

Some were in shock. Not everyone met the Master and yet, here she was, one was thinking.

Another, a boy near the back, was thinking that he needed to record this and use it as his school project. She grinned since that type of innovative thinking was exactly what Eons needed.

One right in the front row was shielding her thoughts, repeating a children's nursery rhyme over and over to hide her thoughts, and she stared at the Master, challenging her to see through the rhyme. Gloria smiled at this one and reached out to touch her arm. Direct contact between Issians meant that a brain-to-brain connection was made, and no Issian could hide from direct contact. She smiled again at the girl as she dropped her hand.

She looked at the boy in the back row of teenagers. "If you'd like, young man, you may come out to the walled city, and I would be more than pleased to sit with you for a real interview for your school project," she said.

That got a gasp from the young man as he more than nodded his head.

She turned to the girl on the left edge of the group and smiled at her too. "Yes, I know that many Issians do not get to meet the Master—and as the new Master Adept, I can promise that I will be here often, many times a month, to meet anyone who would like to meet me. Please, pass that along to your friends and families," she said.

As she prepared to walk on, she looked at the girl in the front row who was still reciting that rhyme over and over and she shook her head at her. "Miss, my advice is to tell your parents immediately. Today. Tell them today, and you may also add that the Master has looked forward and there are only good things to come of this. You have my word," she said, and she walked on with her aide.

The girl had found out that she was pregnant just this morning and didn't know what to do. Her support system, Gloria knew, began with her parents—so that's where she should start. She really had no idea what would happen, but as there were millions of people on Eons, births happened daily, so one more would not be a real problem, especially if the girl would come clean to her parents.

They walked on. They met many more citizens. Many stood in awe. Some were too surprised or in shock to speak while others rhymed their way into anonymity. She didn't really have much to do for these few hours but to meet her citizens.

She enjoyed it, actually, and while it was a part of what her new duties were going to be as the Master, she didn't really think of it as a chore.

She smiled as the robo-cab door closed behind her and her aide gave instructions to the Issian walled city about fifteen miles north of Dessau.

She watched as the city core went by, then the streets got emptier, and the robo-cab sped up until they were on the main road home. She saw the brown walls coming up as they got closer, and at the entrance gate, her aide helped her out, and made their way to the tower and her rooms.

"Still need to work on other issues," she said to herself, "such as the Praix and what would come of the new discovery of their technology over on Ghayth ..."

She was glad she'd at least had some time to herself between the sleeper ships out to the RIM and now. This was like being in a cryonic tank, except she wasn't. There was no sleep nor did she have the dreams she'd begun to like in her years of travel to get here.

Instead, she was now stuck in a jail cell, and she didn't have to look around much to see what her existence entailed here on Neres.

There was the bed—a think pallet of a mattress on a concrete pad. It wasn't springy at all, and the coldness of the concrete bled through the thin mattress and always made her cold. There was no bedding either. No pillow, no sheets, and no blankets. Just the mattress.

Over on the far side was her bathroom. Well, as much as a concrete toilet could be. She couldn't even flush it, as the cell AI did that as soon as she stood up after relieving herself.

And on the third wall was the doorway. A solid piece of heavy steel, it glowed blue since it was protected by a force field too. There was no way to even tap on it, never mind trying to break the door down.

The last wall was blank. There was nothing else. No windows to look out of. No vid screen to watch a show or to listen to the news. No paper or any kind of materials to write or draw. She had nothing to do. She felt she would die from boredom.

Her outfit was the same as all prisoners here in

the Barony wing of the Neres City jail wore. A simple one-piece orange jumpsuit. No zipper, of course, but a simple Velcro strip ran from her neck to her groin.

And that was it.

She'd long ago lost track of time, but she'd begun to use the change of meals as a way to try to guess how long she'd been held here. One meal was obviously breakfast as it always came with a fruit juice. Then there were two more meals, which were usually different and not too bad in a few cases. But the fruit juice meal meant a new day.

So far, since she'd begun her counting, there had been fifty-nine juice meals. All she had to do was to remember the number, fifty-nine this time, until the next juice meal. A low-tech answer but it worked.

Plus, while it was hard to tell as the lights in her cell never varied, in her mind, the time between the third meal of the day and the next juice meal was a long time. It was then that she tried to sleep.

But that was hard to accomplish as her mind continued to work, churning with her failure. She had come all this way over years and years to do one thing—avenge her sister Nora by killing Tanner Scott, the man who had killed her.

He was her brother, but that meant nothing to her. The Branton courts had found him guiltless in Nora's death, which also meant nothing. Her mother had known that Tanner had sacrificed Nora, which meant everything.

She'd killed two others by mistake, but that meant nothing to her. She had not killed Tanner Scott, and that meant something. She sat on her bed and contemplated her failure.

Moving off the bed to start her push-ups, she pumped out fifty-nine in a row. She then rolled over and did three sets of fifty-nine crunches, her feet pressed up tightly against the concrete bed to get some leverage on her abs. She then stood and did five sets of fifty-nine jumping jacks, working up a sweat too, which was good.

She sat then and as her breathing got back to normal, she thought of one thing and one thing only. If they were holding her, she was going to get a trial perhaps or a hearing. And if Tanner were present, she would get to him and kill him.

It was what she had to do … what she'd promised her mother she would do … and what Nora would expect.

CHAPTER TWO

She walked all the way down the long corridor with her heels slamming on the tiles; a mad Baroness was something to behold, and not a single servant, aide, or EliteGuard could be seen. They know well enough to leave me alone, she thought, and she turned at the big marble doorway and went into her own private study to drop into her chair at her desk.

Her husband had told her that the desk itself was worth a frigate in price as it was over a thousand years old and had come from a world inward more than five thousand lights away. She remembered nodding at the time and trying to look interested, but right now, she was more than upset with the Caliph and the chairman too.

Caliph Sharia al Dotsa, the head of the Caliphate

on the RIM, had a realm of only nine planets. Her
own Barony had ten, which would soon be eleven
when Ghayth would be granted full membership.
But with all of its casinos, the Caliphate was still
one of the richest realms in the Confederacy.
Gambling was something that somehow struck a
nerve in every single species that happened upon it.
It didn't matter if aliens or humans were throwing
the dice or pulling the slot machine levers.
Everyone liked to win, and as the only RIM
Confederacy realm with casinos on almost a
hundred worlds or space stations, the Caliphate
capitalized on the players' losses. Gambling had
never appealed to her, but she knew there were
millions of gamblers on Neres itself, all hoping to
roll a seven.

She snorted.

The Caliph had refused to take her EYES ONLY
call, and she had a feeling it was because he knew
she was going to ask point-blank if the Caliphate
was on the Duchy d'Avigdor's list. Over the past
few years, she thought she had been able to forge at
least a working pro-tem partnership with the alien.
He seemed to want what she wanted. She had
recognized that, and she had been cautiously
tempting him with more every year. Now, the
Ikarian vaccine, which would double the lifespan of
anyone who took the single dose of same, was in his

hands. She'd ensured that the Caliph had more than enough of the pre-release samples for his own use and to give to family too. In his realm, one could have a plethora of wives, and the rumor he had more than a hundred wives might be true, so she had provided the Caliph with an adequate amount of the vaccine.

She snorted again.

The question was, could one could pay enough attention to more than one spouse to keep the marriage based on love and affection positive. Of course, she thought, some of us have trouble with just one—a hundred times less—and isn't that the truth.

She shook her head. She kicked off her heels and rested one calf on the corner of her desk as she leaned back to think. Her toes were still polished with a crimson color from Carnarvon. Her retinue included a great girl from Veloka, the capital city on Carnarvon. When she returned from her last trip home, she had brought some polishes in colors the Baroness had never seen before. This crimson had highlights of blue in it, and when the light hit a toe just right, the polish glowed. In her open-toed heels, she often noticed the men around her looked at her feet much more often than they looked at her chest.

She grinned and made a mental note to give the girl from Carnarvon some kind of nice gift. She was as rich as anyone on the RIM, but the gift ould need to be in balance with the act itself. In the past, she had given gifts as a tip, and the value of the gifts had far exceeded the value of the service provided. She remembered that had caused her no end of trouble.

Suitable, she thought. She wanted a suitable and tactful tip. A case of wine—not the ten thousand credits per bottle vintage but the fifty credits per bottle vintage—would be suitable. Who'd even drink that low-level dishwater was beyond her, but it was a normal gift item.

She sighed. Being a Baroness—when you were born dirt poor and raised that way—was difficult and required much growth. "I've done my best so far, but there is room to grow even more," she said to herself as she flexed her toes one way and then the other to see the blue glow for herself.

Back to the list, she thought, and the second alien she was mad at.

Gramsci of Alex'n, the realm in the Confederacy with fifteen planets, was the chairman and head of the RIM Confederacy Council. She was the vice chairman and she was aiming at growing the Barony to surpass that number and take over as the full chairman of the Confederacy. It was her goal, but to do that, she'd need to think about more than just an EYES ONLY. The Caliph had evaded her, and the chairman, while he'd taken the call, had offered up not a single thing to help her. All six of his arms he'd held palms up to show that he had no idea. Honestly, he'd even said.

She hadn't learned if the Alex'n empire was on the list; the chairman was too smart for that kind of a mistake. She'd asked him point-blank, and he denied it. He'd said that his realm was quite happy with fifteen worlds and that someone, yes, he'd imagined, would take over the Duchy d'Avigdor. He had no idea who that might be, he'd said.

He was lying, she thought. He must have an idea and if he knew of the list, then he'd know the Barony was on it too.

Not willing to help at all, she thought as she toyed with the edge of her desk pad, worrying a fingernail into the seam of the leather. She looked out the window to her left and noted the always sunny day and the blue, blue sky with a few wispy clouds were there as always. Neres had exceptionally good weather, and the seasons were pretty much the same as the planet had a tilt of only four percent. During winter, the temperatures only dropped about five degrees or so.

She looked down to the horizon that lay to the west of the Barony Palace and noted the huge towers of Neres City a few miles distant. From here, she could not see much more than the skyscrapers and towers of the core of the city, and yet, it always seemed to calm her somewhat.

She was mad. No doubt about that, but in reality, she was mad at herself. Whatever had made her think that just asking if a realm was on the duchy's list would work was wrong. It would take more than that.

If she could find out who was on the list, and work against them, she had a better chance of the list shrinking to finally have only one realm on it.

The Barony.

She smiled at that. Ten plus six equals sixteen planets, and according to the RIM Confederacy, the head of state of the largest realm on the RIM took over as the chairman of the RIM Council.

That was her goal. But how to get there, she wondered, and more importantly, how to get rid of her competitors quickly was the question of the day ...

Walking across the sand, an EliteGuardsman approached Tanner and Helena and stopped just short of Tanner. It was another sunny day with cool ocean breezes on Bottle, and Tanner and Helena were in their usual spot lying on a chaise lounge below a huge orange umbrella with a sweet and sour punch cocktail at hand.

The EliteGuard cleared his throat, and Tanner lifted his head and turned to his left to see the man standing at attention in the bright sun. EliteGuards dressed in full uniform at all times, but that was something he'd look into later—after the honeymoon. The black and china blue uniforms with those spit-and-polished blue boots and the large twin crowns logo of the Barony on the left side of the chest with the military-style full collar must be hot, he thought.

"Yes ... what's up?" he said, holding a hand over his brow to help dim the glare off the ocean a bit.

"My Lord—an unusual occurrence. We have had a ship from Neen in the Duchy d'Avigdor arrive— with a credentialed ambassador on board who says he needs to speak to you. He offered up no information about why or what his business was— and even us saying that we were under strict privacy orders to deny anyone access to the honeymoon couple would not make him leave.

"They've been sitting on the landing port now for over twenty-one hours, and they said they have no intention of leaving 'til he gets to speak to Lord Scott, My Lord."

The EliteGuard was nervous. Strict privacy orders was one way to put it—Helena had said, months ago, that anyone who broke that would end up digging ore over on ITO for the rest of their lives. For this guard—a major, Tanner could see by his gold oak leaves on his collar—to come out to tell them this was unusual indeed.

He nodded to the guard, waved him away, and turned to Helena. "Looks like life is intruding—but it's the duchy, and it may be about the duke or something. Could I see him?" he asked nicely.

She held up her palm, the edge on her brow to see in the reflected glare off the waters, and grinned at him.

"Lord Scott has no need to ask anyone ever for permission to do anything, dear. Well, maybe to change the furniture in our new bedroom—the choice of what you want to do, Tanner, is yours. I'm gonna have another of those punch drinks, and I think I'll ask the chef for a light fresh fish dinner this evening—okay, honey?" she said as she leaned back into the lounge chair.

He grinned at her, though she couldn't see it, and said, "I'll get your drink ordered and be back soon as I hear the ambassador." He hoisted himself up and out of the lounge. As comfortable as they were, these lounge chairs were a real pain to get up and out of, and as he used his left hand to grip the left arm, he felt the tightness around his left clavicle and where it met the sternum.

When the shooting at his wedding had occurred, a bullet had driven into his chest and cracked his sternum, which had pushed the bullet to the left side of his heart as it grazed the left ventricle and caused his heart to spasm. If it wasn't for one of his groomsmen, who was a medical doctor, and being within fifty feet of a mobile robo-doc, Tanner might not have made it.. But now, after more than two months of careful rest and relaxation, it was apparent to him that while he was healed, there would always be some stiffness and pain when he moved to his left.

He grinned for a moment. If some pain getting out of a chair on Bottle was the only price he paid for the assassination attempt, then he was truly a lucky man. Correct that, he thought as his grin widened, a lucky lord.

He stood and stretched. He saw the EliteGuard back up off the beach, near the small pool and bar, and he made his way up the slightly sloping sand and joined him.

"Major, I'll see the ambassador. Please let them know and have him—and whomever else he wants to bring along—come down here to the bar," he said.

The guard snapped him a salute, said, "Yes, My Lord," and rushed off.

Tanner looked over at the bartender who doubled as their steward. "Could you please take another of those excellent punch drinks down to the lady for me, please—and then give me some privacy here at the bar?"

The bartender was soon a mixing and pouring at light speed. Tanner sat on one of the stools and turned back to face the waters.

On Bottle, the ocean was massive. So big, the locals claimed, that there were probably islands with societies and people that had never seen others before. He knew the planet mapping showed more than eighty thousand islands, atolls, keys, and the like, as well as the three major continents too. An audit report by the Barony team that had put together the proposal to buy this resort had agreed with the locals' claim.

The three major continents were lightly populated too, which was an issue. As a single planet with no real salable economy, they would not survive for long. To resolve the issue, Bottle had become a tourist island. It marketed water and beaches for relaxing vacations, and with the raw undeveloped beauty of the beaches and oceans, it had survived.

"Lord Scott. May I sit please, My Lord?" a voice over his shoulder said.

He turned to look at the man who'd spoken. He was about six feet tall with white hair and looked about eighty years old. He had blue eyes—really piercing blue eyes—under white brows. He was in pretty good shape too, and he'd dressed for the beach — well, at least he had on an un-tucked short-sleeved shirt with his slacks and he wore sandals too.

"Yes, I'm Tanner Scott — you're?" he answered, noting the ambassador had come alone.

Normally he would have held out his hand, but both his new wife and the Baroness had reprimanded him — Royals never did that unless the person was a very loyal, well-known friend.

"Ambassador Bedre, My Lord. I have been in the Duchy Diplomatic Corps for over fifty years, and I have recently been appointed as the head of the Duchy Provisional Government, well, until our future has been decided," he said.

His voice was smooth with tones that, to Tanner at least, indicated decades of speaking to all types in his diplomatic career. It was, Tanner thought, very much like speaking to his friend Ambassador Harmon, who he'd gotten to know those few years back when the planet Enki had been admitted to the RIM Confederacy.

Using your voice as a tool was something most people never even considered, yet Tanner knew this was not only a tool to a diplomat — but often a weapon. I'd be smart to go lightly here, he thought as he nodded to the man.

"Ambassador, welcome to Bottle. What is it that I

can do for you—and also, what might be so important that you'd interrupt a man's honeymoon?" he asked.

That set the ambassador back on his heels. "My Lord, I apologize for that, but it is not my own doing. I am here today on strictly confidential grounds, as I obey one of the duke's—rather the late duke's—codicils in his will. This was demanded of me. I do apologize, My Lord," he said.

Now Tanner was the one taken aback somewhat. He leaned over to his right and stared over at the bartender who'd just returned from delivering the fresh punch to his wife. Tanner gestured that he'd like one too, and once again, the mixing machine began to blend all the ingredients into a frothy foam. The bartender presented the drink and then left the bar area.

Tanner took a healthy pull on the double straws and got a good-sized mouthful of sweet and sour fruity punch. He was going to call the bartender back and offer the ambassador one—then he cut that off. No better way to remind the man which one of them was Royalty than to not share his hospitality. "I see, Ambassador. So what is it that you've come to say?"

The ambassador nodded, but it was more like he dipped his head with a teensy bow, maybe, Tanner thought.

"My Lord, the duke—sorry, the late duke—
added a new codicil to his will only three months
ago. It outlines what he wanted done—should he
not get to do it himself during his lifetime. As he
was a ... victim of the shooting just those two
months ago, the will was read right after that to a
closed session of the Provisional Duchy
Government's cabinet just two weeks ago. At that
time, and after much advice from our legal
department and even from some selected RIM
Confederacy constitutional experts, I was charged
with the duty to bring the late duke's wishes to you
for you to hear them. And for you to decide, My
Lord."

He slid a small bag off his shoulder, laid it on the
bar to Tanner's left, and placed a hand on it. "Inside
this is the duke's will—we would ask please that it
be kept confidential, My Lord. And there is a
marker on the pages that concern this new codicil
and how it might affect you—and your life too, My
Lord. You have been bequeathed something ..." he
said.

His voice sounded almost normal, but Tanner
thought he could detect a small tone of anxiety
almost hidden away behind the words. He put a
hand down on the corner of the leather bag and
half-smiled back at the ambassador.

"And what exactly did the duke leave me?" he asked as he sipped again on his punch.

"He left you the duchy, My Lord. You are — or you can be — the new Duke d'Avigdor," the ambassador said, his voice now open and honest.

Tanner spit up the partially swallowed fruit punch all over the bar ...

#####

He really didn't know what the major cause was of his newly found impatience, but it was there anyways.

He had a sister in the Barony cells, charged with assassinating the Master Adept and the Duke d'Avigdor and wounding him at the same time.

Yesterday, he had been presented with the duke's will and had read carefully the codicil about what might become his future — should he wish to become the new duke and rule the Duchy d'Avigdor and its six planets.

He had been lying on that chaise lounge for more than two months, soaking up the sun, resting and relaxing, and finding it harder and harder to get up and out of that chair too.

He needed a gym — not a halfhearted attempt at a gym like the few machines over in the commons room area. A real gym full of marines would get him to rev up his now fatter body and get back into shape. He went off on a tangent thinking about how difficult it was to get back into shape now that he was over forty, but he brought his train of thought back to what lay ahead of him.

He smiled at Helena. Must do this, he thought, and he grinned at her with what he hoped was his best smile.

"Okay," she said, as she put down her fork and reached for the glass of white wine in front of her. She sipped the wine, cupped it in front of her, and smiled back as she said, "Out with it, Lord Scott!"

How she knew he had something to say was truly beyond him, but then he nodded as he realized she knew him pretty damn well.

He set down his fork, the fish entree forgotten, raised his glass of white wine, and toasted her. "To my wife—who knows me better than I know myself. Care to tell me what I'm about to say?" he said nicely.

She nodded. "You want to get back to reality— you are healed, and you have made up your mind on what to do with your sister," she said, her voice not quite flat and empty of emotion.

He caught that, so he tried to tell her how he felt. "Honey, yes, I do wish to get back to reality. But what to do with Gia is, as yet, beyond me. For now, sitting in a cell will do fine, I'd think. No, it's the duchy thing that has me thinking ..." he finished off, and she just stared back at him.

Last night after the Duchy d'Avigdor's ambassador had left at dinner, he'd simply handed her the duke's will—earmarked where it talked about him—and he'd sat back.

She'd read it. Then she'd reread it, put it down, and continued to eat. She had said nothing.

He'd waited.

She had taken a couple of bites of her dinner, and then, like just a few minutes ago, she had dropped her fork and picked up her wine.

She'd talked to him about the Barony and how she could never ever be anything but the Baroness —true to her heritage, she'd called it. Without any malice in her tone, she had said the duke's kind offer was up to him—but she would be the Baroness one day and that was that. He thought maybe she had meant "choose me and the Barony."

He'd sat at that point, for almost five minutes, and then he'd loudly announced an answer she had never thought of herself. "May I present the Duchess of d'Avigdor, the Baroness of Neres, Helena St. August," he intoned as if he were introducing her at a formal state event.

She started, spilling her wine a bit. She hadn't considered that she could be both. She smiled back widely, and he knew she was on board.

He had gone on to let her know that the baroness

who married a duke would, of course, get the title of duchess. She'd have the job of being the head of state of the Barony as well as his ducal consort too. And after some time, the Barony would grow to include the duchy ... something that was dawning on her now.

She smiled at him. "And I know a guy too ... the best constitutional expert here on the RIM. One Professor Klaasjan Boven of the university on Carnarvon—he was at the Halberd anniversary event on the stage—do you remember him?" she asked

He shook his head. "Not hardly ... that was a day I try to never, ever remember," he said quietly and looked off toward the blue of the ocean.

She had looked off into the distance too, at the far horizon, where the calm ocean blended into the ocean deeps. She had a small smile on her face reminding him that the codicil had some other things to think about.

He had nodded back, and they'd gone back to the delicious fish dinner.

"Thinking what," she said, interrupting his recollection of last night and bringing him back to tonight.

He nodded. "Gia. I'm thinking of what to do with her. Death for her crimes I do not countenance at all—she was brainwashed by our mother that I killed Nora—which I did not do. But to carry that kind of hate for all these years and then find me and come out to the RIM to kill me—I cannot imagine what kind of a messed-up psyche she must have. But—she is blood, and I can't forget that either, yet she took two innocent lives ..." he said.

She nodded as she took a sip of the buttery soft chardonnay.

He went on, thinking out loud as he did. "So, what I think I'm going to do—with your approvals, of course—is to sentence her to life imprisonment but mitigate that by making her a patient up on our Hospital Ship over Neres. I will assign her the same team that I had—and hopefully, the doctors there can help her see her errors and mis-thinking and cure her of that at least," he said.

Helena leaned forward to clasp his hand. "Honey, you don't need my approvals at all— you're Lord Scott. Command, and it will be done. But I do have one question, Tanner—what will you do if, in time, the doctors pronounce her cured? Commute her sentence?" she asked.

He took a sip of his wine which turned into a big gulp, and he shrugged.

"I've no idea. Would be years, I'd think, so no need to decide anything as yet. Oh," he added after a second's pause, "will we need to have a real public trial and all?"

Helena shrugged as she answered. "Not really, as your Lord Scott. Command and it's done ... but there are millions of Eons and Neen citizens who might like to see the assassin of their heads of state get that trial, be found guilty, and sentenced. Might be the best way to give them closure, Tanner?" she asked.

He nodded.

"True. Let's do that then," he said, and he picked up his glass again.

"Could I ask," Helena said, "that we stay just one more day? I'll notify the staff that we're leaving the day after tomorrow, bound for Neres City?"

He nodded once again and smiled at her. The wine went down nicely as he hoped he'd actually made a good decision about the future of his assassin sister ...

#####

The news came in as usual, via an EYES ONLY, to the head of the Hospital Ship over Neres, and as soon as it was over, messages for the team to assemble in the administrative meeting room were sent out by the chief of medicine for the Barony Hospital Ship, Doctor Zacrom Mendoza. It took almost thirty minutes, but eventually Maddie was able to close the door to ensure privacy, and she nodded to Mendoza that all were there.

He looked around the room and half-smiled at them all. "I was just on an EYES ONLY with Lord Scott—our own patient of a year ago or so—and I have some interesting news as well as a caution for you all," he said.

Doctor Craig Nelson, the head of family medicine and a general practitioner of some stature, was agitated a bit, and he leaned forward. "Doctor, could we not have just gotten an IM on this? I have patients to attend to—as I'm sure we all do," he said as he looked around the large conference room on Deck Twenty-four for support.

Doctor Lathan Trystan, who was the head of the group sessions department, nodded. "We've got another session starting in like twenty minutes, Doctor Mendoza ... so ..." he said.

Maddie, the nurse practitioner who acted as the meeting secretary nodded, and the only other person in the room, Doctor Etter, the psychiatrist, sat silently without moving.

"Fine," Mendoza said, "then in a nutshell, here's what the half hour EYES ONLY was all about. We're getting Gia Scott, the girl who assassinated the Master Adept and the Duke d'Avigdor, as a patient. She will be held in the strictest of modes here, and she will be treated by you three. Maddie, for all the normal orientation to the Hospital Ship; Doctor Nelson, you'll be her general practitioner;

Doctor Trystan will have her in his groups; and
Doctor Etter, you will look after her psyche.
Clear?" he said and leaned back.

Surprised, everyone in the group, except Maddie,
sat back and did not make a sound.

Maddie leaned forward in her seat. "Doctor
Mendoza, might I inquire as to why we were
picked for this—and in fact why the patient is not
just going to be tried in a court and found guilty?"
she asked.

He nodded. "That's the part that is the easiest to
answer. Lord Scott instructed me—that as you all
were in charge of his ninety-day observation time
awhile back—that you'd be the best ones to do this.
He felt—and I think his reasoning is sound here—
that you'd all bring something extra to the table as
you have already studied him. He thinks—please
keep this confidential—that his sister is what he
called brainwashed and she was acting as she'd
been trained by her mother. Lord Scott's mother
too, I'd add, and I think that Doctor Etter will need
to consider much to come up with a diagnosis," he
said.

Everyone nodded, and he checked the tablet on
the table in front of him. "She arrives the day after
tomorrow. Normal check-ins—all of you to attend
same—and, Maddie, she is to be put into Lord
Scott's old room, E-217. He was quite specific on

that—and that his own time here should be shared with her, if needs be. She is to be implanted with a chip—we need to know where she is at all times, and that's a certainty. I expect you all to remember that while we all saw—some of us closer than others"—he looked over at Doctor Etter—"that she committed a horrendous crime in killing those two at Lord Scott's wedding, she is a criminal second and our patient first as our oath stipulates," he finished and smiled at them all.

"Questions?" he asked.

Maddie shook her head. Doctor Nelson and Doctor Etter also shook their heads.

Doctor Trystan, however, did have one. "Is she to go into the mix for group? Can I add her, I mean, to any of same, or is there to be special treatment— after all, she is Lord Scott's sister ..." he asked, his eyebrows raised.

Doctor Mendoza shook his head. "No special treatment—treat her like any patient needing our help. But a reminder—I need weekly reports on your interim prognosis for her all the time she's with us. And a gentle reminder to keep them very medical, as they will all be forwarded to Lord Scott on his orders, too."

While he didn't say it, they all knew that meant that any subjective comments by any of them would need to be backed up medically—it would keep the gut instinct opinions to a minimum, which sometimes were counter-intuitive to good healthcare. The meeting broke up a few minutes later.

CHAPTER THREE

This time, the hallway outside the RIM Confederacy Council chambers had only a hint of water from the recent DenKoss members' tanks, Admiral McQueen thought as he carefully picked his way down the tile hallway. *Whomever had invented tile floors, he* thought, *should have thought about what happened with a bit of water on same and how you could go head over heels in a split-second.*

He shook his head at the stray thought. There are more important fish to fry today, and he continued on his way to the monthly Council meeting. As he gingerly turned the corner into the room, one of the Provost guards nodded at him and waved him to one side as he was carefully mopping up the water. "Good to see," McQueen said to himself as the uproar over a Council member slipping on the tile was not a good thing at all. He remembered the to-do a few years back about a Council member slipping on the tile.

He shrugged, went around the huge Council table to his left, and nodded to some of the members already seated at the table. He noted that a large white-haired man sat in the late duke's chair. He knew he'd meet the man filling in for the Duke d'Avigdor later, and he nodded to others as he went past the head of the table.

Behind the table itself, in tiered seating rows, his own seat was at the front of the section reserved for Confederacy departments. As the admiral in charge of the RIM Confederacy Navy, he sat just to the left and behind the Council chairman. He dropped his papers and files and his tablet, which he swore got heavier as the number of files on it grew. He made his way over to the new Master Adept who was already seated on the right-hand side of the enormous horseshoe-shaped table. He smiled at her and she rose—somewhat unusual for her to do so—but he bowed his head to the Issian.

"Ma'am, good to finally meet you and to say hello before the meeting starts. Might I add that the Confederacy Navy is so proud of what you've built on Eons for the naval academy and in record time too," he said. And he was right, he knew, that the academy was up and running and now housed almost six thousand cadets, all enrolled to become naval officers after graduation.

She smiled at him, returned the bow, and spoke softly so that only he could hear her in the busy room. "Admiral—yes, so nice to meet you finally. And might I say that your own help, along with the other admirals and Lord Scott too, to aid us in getting the academy finished and launched on time was very much the foundation of our success," she said. She held out her hand too, and he shook it gently, a bit surprised at her grip too. Strong and hearty was her style, it appeared.

"We should talk often and about many things," he said. He grinned at her. He grinned at her. "And about the academy too," he said pointedly.

She tilted her head to one side, as she looked into his mind. Moments later, she nodded. "I will make myself available whenever you can meet, Admiral, but until then, be advised that the duchy presentation today concerns Lord Scott. I thought you should know," she said. Being able to read a mind was an Issian characteristic that she more than understood, and the admiral did not have to speak his thoughts to her out loud. The Duchy d'Avigdor and Lord Scott appeared to be the topic, and he smiled back at her.

"I will contact you tomorrow to see when we can meet, Master Adept, if that suits? And I thank you too," he said and got a nod in return.

A flurry of latecomers to the Council chamber suddenly came in, and the Admiral nodded and returned to take his seat. The latecomers, from Faraway, Novertag, Ttseen, Farth, and Skogg had all arrived and were taking their seats when the last missing Council members, the Baroness and Chairman Gramsci both took their seats as well.

"Call to order, please, " the clerk said as she rose from her seat in the area in the middle of the horseshoe table.

Chairman Gramsci, the head of state of Alex'n, the largest realm in the Confederacy, banged a gavel with one hand, juggled file folders with two more, scratched his ear with another, and tapped his fingers on the tablet in front of him all at the same time. Having six hands was the best thing about the Alex'n aliens and was a well-known fact. But as usual, it gave them little advantage in a meeting. Maybe it is better in situations where manual dexterity is important, the admiral thought.

"Order, please ... order. Clerk, any regrets for this meeting?" he asked.

She nodded to him as she glanced over to the left-hand wall and the large display of the table and the members seated so far today.

"We do have regrets from Carnarvon—they will miss this meeting due to a series of heavy thunderstorms with rains that are causing major issues with some of their coastal cities. We wish them well. All others," she said as she pointed at the icons around the table on the screen that were green—only the Carnarvon one was red, "are present and accounted for.

"Small point, though, Mr. Chairman, that the Duke d'Avigdor, of course, is not present. In his place is Ambassador Bedre, the head of the Duchy Provisional Government, acting in that capacity." She pointed out the ambassador.

Ambassador Bedre nodded and smiled.

Chairman Gramsci thanked the clerk for the notices and said, "Agenda, please, Clerk"

"Mr. Chairman, yes, Agendas were distributed, and all items there are ready for discussion. Please hold new business until the end of the meeting as is our usual way," she answered, and she sat to begin to record the meeting.

Admiral McQueen was not so much interested in the bulk of the Agenda items, but he was more than a little interested in the Duchy d'Avigdor item and the fact that the ambassador would be making a presentation on it soon. It was item number four, but still, there was a bunch to wade through to get to that item. He sighed to himself and half-smiled to the room.

First up was the general point on the recent trade

wars between Leudi and Faraway. A summary of their current positions was made by both the Leudi and Faraway Council members. Amazing how in sync they were and how ninety-five percent of their issues had disappeared once push had come to shove. Each had threatened to leave the RIM Confederacy if they didn't gain supremacy over the other, which would have meant much hardship, economically and culturally, for all the realms on the RIM.

But the Baroness had quelled that in one act: giving the Barony Drive—instant travel anywhere —to RIM Confederacy members only. With the ability to now go from UrPoPo to Randi, more than eighty lights apart, in seconds, the cost of shipping and trading had been too much for the two trading races to bear. They'd "folded their tents in the night" and the previously partisan-based planets had complied to find ways to compete without triggering a trade war.

He ducked his head as he remembered that the number of protests in one of his departments had gone from more than a thousand to less than a dozen in two days. All had been rescinded and all had been done away with. The Barony Drive worked for us all, he thought as he began to listen in to the discussion.

The Council moved on to item number two, the

new academy on Eons. With more than 1300 graduating naval cadets—soon to be second lieutenants—the pipeline of new naval officers was about up to where it should be. With more than ninety planets in the forty-realm Confederacy, navies were always looking for more officers, so this was a good thing.

There were more than two hundred new naval ships in the Confederacy, which was also a sign that the RIM was both alive and doing well. New naval officers were needed for sure, the admiral thought.

The member from Eran, the Nizami himself, didn't bother to rise to speak. At twelve feet in height, this head of state was more than impressive. He said, "Not enough 'accommodations' have been made to the academy to allow us to send through officer candidates in any large numbers."

He was right, the admiral knew, as the academy could at this point handle only twenty-five Erans. With them being twice the height of normal humans and aliens, that meant separate larger-sized dorm rooms, classroom seats, computer desks, and more, and currently, there were only twenty-five each of all the necessary items in the larger size.

The Nizami continued, keeping a polite tone in his voice. "Next year, we'd like to double the size of our candidates."

That received a consensus around the table. The

member from Hope said, "If that means more 'accommodations' would need to be made, then so be it. I'd vote aye for those changes right now."

Moved by the Nizami and seconded by the Hope member, the idea was quickly passed. It went to the Confederacy and the Eons members to work out the details and get back to the Council by next meeting with a timeline and a budget too.

Done, the Admiral thought and looked down at his Agenda. Oh, the Ikarian vaccine is next.

The Baroness rose, and the room instantly quieted. The woman who ran the Barony realm was human, and all agreed she was one of the most beautiful women on the RIM. Dressed today in a shade of teal and deep green, the woman certainly knew how to look impressive. Her golden hair and haloed her beauty. Her nails, he noted, had a glint of blue behind some sort of polished crimson. More than enough woman for any man, thought, or maybe too much for most.

She looked around the room and the small talk ended. "I come before you today," she said nicely, "to report that we have been successful in finding an answer to the Ikarian vaccine." She half-turned to point behind her. There, sitting in the bottom tier, was Ahanu, the Ikarian member who represented his planet of Throth.

Ahanu was tall with jet-black hair and his

piercing blue eyes took in all around him. Wearing a leather jerkin and a large beaded necklace, he looked like a warrior, there was no doubt about that, and even though he appeared to be unarmed, the admiral knew he would be a formidable foe.

Ahanu smiled at them. H dipped his head but then held up his right hand, clasped into a fist, and placed the back of that hand on his forehead in the traditional Ikarian sign of respect.

"Ahanu is an Ikarian—the representative of Throth—who helped to bring his race to our Confederacy. As you all know," the Baroness said as she turned back to fully face the table, "we worked on this for almost four years. And we can now offer up to the RIM Confederacy members that the vaccine, which captures the virus, gives what we think is a doubled lifetime to anyone who simply drinks the single dose.

"Our testing continues, and we're up to," she said as she glanced down at the tablet in front of her, "more than an eighty-one percent success rate for all. That is, for eighty-one out of every one hundred races, human or alien, our testing has proved, the vaccine will double their lifetime range. If you should live to be one hundred and twenty, then our vaccine should double that to two hundred and forty years, all things being taken into account.

"Might we ask," the Caliph interrupted her, "if it

works on all our Confederacy races? Each of our alien and human ones?" he queried.

The Baroness nodded. "Yes, it works for all. In fact, we've, as yet, not found a race that it does not work on ..." she said nicely.

She knows what is coming next, the admiral thought.

"And can we inquire as to what this will cost us Confederacy members? With more than a billion citizens in the Caliphate, the costs are very much an important factor for us," the Caliph went on.

The admiral looked around to catch many nods from many of the members.

"Yes, Caliph, we intend to sell the vaccine — to Confederacy members only — at cost. That would be less than four credits per dose, at least at our current manufacturing levels. Should we ramp up our production and find cost efficiencies — the price to you would go down. We do not look at the vaccine as a 'cash-cow,' so to speak — rather as a way to enrich the whole RIM Confederacy."

That got silence in the room. Each of the members was multiplying their number of citizens times four to come up with a cost for them to adopt the vaccine realm-wide.

"And should we, say, buy a million doses and then offer them for sale on our own planets at a markup, would that be allowed?" the Caliph went on.

"We do not have a problem with that," the Baroness said, "as long as you're aware that it would be available on every single commercial ship, space stations, and the like all at the four credits per dose, base price," she said.

Bingo, the admiral thought. So should the Caliph, say, try to charge twenty credits or a hundred credits per dose, the population would simply find another outlet at the base cost.

The Caliph stared at her, his face frozen with no expression.

"So," the Baroness said, "we roll out the vaccine as of tomorrow. Please just place any orders with our new vaccine order department," she said as she sat and smiled at them all.

Interesting, the admiral thought. The greatest thing to come to the RIM — so for four credits, he could live to be two hundred or so. He'd spend the four credits, he knew, as would, he thought, every single other member here.

"Item number four. The presentation of the Duchy d'Avigdor by Ambassador Bedre," the clerk read.

The admiral leaned in to get a feel for what was to come. *A realm of six planets with no head of state was something that hadn't happened before, and this was going to be interesting ...*

 '

#####

Tanner grinned at Helena and squeezed her hand in response to the huge round of applause for them on the landing pad at their resort.

It was time to leave Bottle and get back to the real world, he knew. She had simply nodded and agreed with him a week back as they made their plans as to what to do about many things when they returned. He had smiled at her often over the next few days as he had proposed one thing—and she had to yet again remind him that as a Royal, he wouldn't be doing those kinds of things any more. He would need to find staff to do them. In his mind, he replayed his conversations with Helena about the issues he wanted to address

He wanted to find a real replacement captain for the *Atlas*. She was over off Ghayth, as a part of the xeno team deployment, and right now was under the temporary care of Captain Eleanor Vennamo. He'd pushed that one through back when he'd been admiral, and now he needed to choose what to do with the captaincy. Then Captain Vennamo could go back to the *Gibraltar*, her own ship currently in dry dock for major updates. Helena had reminded him that this task was no longer his but belonged to the admiral of the Barony fleet.

The fact that there was no such admiral was

another task—he'd have to find someone to do that —and he thought he had a great candidate. Of course, that would put the Barony fleet under someone else's control, he'd told Helena, and she'd just shrugged. "No matter," she'd said. "As a Royal, you command."

He'd nodded and then went on with more and more issues. He had been in the process of having brand new buildings contracted over on Neres at the naval yards, and he wanted to find out the status of their development. Helena had shaken her head and said, "New admiral's job."

He wanted to take on more of a role with the Captains Council and formulate new bylaws and such so that each Barony captain knew where they were all the time. "Admiral," Helena said, sipping her drink.

He wanted to go to Ghayth to see the latest findings of the xeno team. He nodded to her when she said that could be accomplished at any time— but it was not behooving of a Royal to check on such a project in person. "Better just take the reports for now," she'd said as she turned over on her hip to reach for more sun butter to rub on her legs.

He wanted to also go back to Neres City, to the naval yards, and scoop up his aide, Lieutenant Ayla Kiraz, and make her a part of his "Lord" staff. He broached that to Helena who was busy rubbing the cream onto her thighs, and she nodded back right away.

"Excellent idea. Finding someone who you can trust as an aide is one of the hardest things to do as a Royal. If you want her, get her. But a short reminder, honey? Taking her out of the mainstream of navy life might mean that she loses out on chances therein. Are you sure you wouldn't be hurting her long-term career?"

He sighed, accepted the sun butter tube, and rubbed a healthy dose of same across his brow and ears too. That would require some discussion, he accepted, and he moved on.

"Bram. I want to help him somehow, yet not tag him as a 'teacher's pet' and yet somehow move him up, naval officer style."

Helena looked off at the far horizon and held a hand across her brow to shade her eyes.

"You know, as far as I can remember, there's never been a Barony captain who's Issian … and we do have, what, six new ships coming online in the next few months. After the Seenra deliver same, they'll all need crew and captains," she said as she returned her arm to her side and relaxed in the bright Bottle sunshine.

He had sighed then and realized that being a Royal was a lot more difficult than he'd imagined.

And today, after packing up their ship, the *Sword*, and getting ready to depart, the whole staff of the resort had stopped him and Helena. They had circled around them, which made the EliteGuardsmen all anxious until they'd been waved away by Helena.

"Lady and Lord, may we just thank you for your time spent here on Bottle," the Concierge said nicely. He moved over to give some hyacinths to Helena, freshly cut and smelling wonderfully. She accepted very politely and smiled at the assembled group of staff. Everyone from chefs to maids, bellmen, gardeners, and pool-boys were there. As well, the administration for the resort, including the resort general manager, had come by to shake their hands and wish them safely home.

"What I can tell you all is that the past few months here with you on Bottle have been about the best form of rest and recuperation for both myself and Lord Scott. As you all know, we came here after that dreadful incident at our wedding— and never have we felt more at home than here on Bottle.

"Once we're gone, as your general manager already knows, there will be more guests vying for rooms here than ever before. We wish you well, and we will be back!" she said, and she dipped her head to them all as a sign of respect.

Tanner had just nodded and led his bride into the *Sword*. On the bridge, he said, "Lieutenant Cooper, back to Nere's City, please, and place her down on the Barony Palace small landing field. We want to go home." He and Helena turned to their right to go down the short corridor to their quarters.

They had just closed the door to their sumptuous quarters and grinned at each other when a chime went off from their AI. Helena walked a few steps to sink into a loveseat of the most wonderful shade of orange, and she waved at him to go ahead.

"Yes, AI," Tanner said, wondering what was so important that the AI had rung them before they'd even lifted off.

"Lord Scott—sorry to interrupt your pleasant trip home, but there is an urgent EYES ONLY that we were told to hold for you. It's from Admiral McQueen, Lord Scott," the AI said.

He looked over at his bride and lifted an eyebrow, and she nodded back to him.

"AI, please play the message here to me, I authorize other eyes," he said, and the AI chimed three times to acknowledge his authorization.

On the close bulkhead wall, a sudden frost of blue wavered into existence, and the blue turned into a full picture of Admiral McQueen as the EYES ONLY began to play.

"Lord Scott—hope you're feeling fine, but I

thought that I should EYES ONLY you as soon as this came to light. At the RIM Confederacy Council meeting in a few days, there was news about the duchy and it's going to be presented by their Ambassador Bedre.

"I have no idea what they're planning to present, but I did want you to know, that it seems that you are a part of it—at least that's what my sources tell me.

"Message me back if you wish, but until the presentation, I've no further news yet, and sorry to somewhat 'muddy' up your honeymoon, lad. Over and out," he finished.

The recorded vid stopped and went back to the blue screen, and then it all winked out.

He looked over at Helena and lifted up a hand, palm open. "So, I thought that the duchy offer was confidential for a year—at least that's what the ambassador said to me."

"You wouldn't be the first Royal to be lied to," she said sweetly, rubbing her mid-thigh to ease the teeniest of sunburns.

He nodded.

If the ambassador did not want him to take over the duchy, this perhaps was one way to attain that goal—make the duke's offer public to create a huge grassroots backlash.

But if the man did want him to take over—then

why do it this way?

Of course, there was no way yet of knowing what the presentation to the Confederacy Council even was, so maybe it was too early to come up with an answer.

He sighed. Being a Royal was a lot more difficult than he'd imagined.

The AI chimed twice, and then a small message appeared on the front-facing bulkhead that read "Leaving Bottle," and while the inertial dampers worked perfectly, he thought that he could feel the ship surge up and spin to port with his "space legs." Using the Barony Drive meant they'd be home on Neres, which was fourteen lights away from Bottle, in a few seconds.

"AI, put the bridge forward screen on, please," he said, and the message disappeared as the *Sword* flew up through the atmosphere of Bottle, and then in low orbit, it slowed to orient itself toward the Neres system. As the star was found and then targeted, the sidebar showed it as their focus, and the sudden growth of the star itself on the screen showed them moving at FTL.

"No sense in getting comfortable," he said as he flopped down beside Helena and smiled at her.

"Lord Scott, I thank you for your time—but you did need to rest and recuperate. Now, it's back to reality," she said, and she sighed too.

#####

She walked a bit quicker as this hallway was somewhat scary to her, but she had checked and there were two EliteGuardsmen just a few steps behind her. She'd never been in this part of the Barony Palace before, and the fact that it was hidden made it seem even scarier. The Baroness shuddered for a second or two.

"Ma'am, are you cold?" one of the guards asked, and she shook her head and continued to follow her aide.

The corridor was carpeted with a deep plush that made their steps disappear. It had no art, photos, or pictures on the walls, which were painted a dark brown that made her think of a cave. There were a few lights on the ceiling, but no fixtures; the naked bulbs hung from wires. It was anything but what one would call attractive or, for that matter, normal.

Yes, normal was the word, she thought. And why should a Baroness—THE Baroness in fact ever have to visit something so dark and dank. Wait, dank meant smelling of water … and that wasn't it either …

She shook her head. Such thoughts are not fit for a Baroness.

They continued walking. They'd begun in the area of the palace where the new wing had been

75

built for Helena and Lord Scott. Making the new wing meld with the much, much older building in that area had meant that the construction crews had to open up a complete set of hallways and rooms that were going to now run directly into the new wing. Seemed like the right thing to do, and she thought she'd nodded a year ago when the plans had to be okayed.

Her aide had informed her that the demolition had revealed a corridor, which was behind all the rooms on one side, the interior side, of the older palace structure. Someone at the time had made notes on that, had explored the whole area, and had made some discoveries. With the huge to-do she called the assassination at the wedding, the gentle apologies, and making all things right with the heads of state, she had put off this trip to see the newly opened area. Until today. And now she was following this aide down a long dark corridor with a few doorways to her left.

On her right was a solid wall, and she'd asked about it a hundred feet back. The aide had shared that this wall was the interior wall of the whole area that held the large conservatory rooms in the palace. The Baroness had spent some time there every so often, but she had never questioned the wall behind the glass-walled plant and root area that let in so much sunshine. She had thought the

wall was just there and hadn't given it a second
thought.

As the corridor up ahead was ending at a
doorway, she shivered and held up a hand to quiet
the EliteGuard behind her. As the aide stopped, she
opened the door and then stepped to one side to
allow her Baroness to go in first. And the Baroness
did just that, entering the darkened room and
taking five big steps ahead.

The room must have been connected to the palace
AI, because just her entry illuminated the whole
room—and it was big. She blinked a couple of
times, and then she gasped at what she saw.

Ahead of her, in very tall glass cases, were
trophies—dead animals that had been somehow
stuffed and then arranged in poses that were
threatening. She knew what a Jael was, and there
was a pair of them in a huge case, each attacking a
common enemy or prey. Beside them were
Garnuthian laxes—cat-like beasts that were big and
strong and fast. Over on the right side was a case
with what looked like weasels, but some looked like
they were five feet at the shoulder and weighed
more than a hundred pounds. Again, she shivered,
and this time it was for what it might be like to face
any of these in a battle for life. She shook her head
and slowly walked around the multitude of glass
cases.

Some had animals that looked like they were from off the RIM. One cabinet was more than twenty feet tall, and the enclosed animal was from a water world—it had fins and a tail, yet it had forearms with huge claws and jaws that held hundreds of teeth. She shuddered. Not the world to go to for a swim, she thought.

One of the cases held what looked almost human-like. Well, maybe alien-like weasel would be more truthful, she thought, wrapping her arms around herself. Its skin looked like polished glass with pearly, pink highlights. The animal had a look on its face as if it were questioning the viewer. The Baroness took a step back and wrapped her arms more tightly around herself as she imagined the creature asking, "Wonder what you'd taste like?"

The creature was more than ten feet tall with enormous, curved, and sharp talons on its rear feet —and there were four of those. The predator had three forearms—two on its left side, and it looked like scars on its right side where it had lost an arm. Its massive teeth and four giant flared nostrils were at odds with the beast's mane of bright pink hair that was thick and curly.

Whatever had taken that one arm was something to stay the hell away from, she thought, and she turned to find her aide.

"Okay … Nancy, right? Okay, Nancy, so what

am I doing here? Trophies are pretty impressive—I suppose that barons before me liked to hunt. So ..." she said. She wasn't tapping her toe, but everyone in the room knew she was impatient for the answer to her question.

"Ma'am, let me just hit this button. Manual control only—at least as far as we know ..." Nancy said as she approached a small kiosk that sat at one side of the rows of glass cabinets. Pushing the button, she stepped back and looked up at the black ceiling.

Above their heads, the RIM suddenly appeared as a star map, lit in bright shades of purple, including lilac, fuchsia, and mauve. The planet that they were on—Neres, the home world of the Baronial realm—was colored red at this point, and the Baroness thought this meant that was where the viewer was. She nodded and then sent a questioning look toward her aide.

The aide nodded, took a few steps to stand in front of the cabinets that held the two Jaels, touched the glass itself, and then she looked up again.

On the star map above them, the world of Anulet, in the Duchy d'Avigdor, suddenly turned red, and the planet jumped up in size. The planet name was there, along with the name of the animal and information about the Jaels too.

She nodded and smiled a bit. "I take it then, that

if you touch the glass of any of these cabinets, their world will show up above us, correct?"

That got a nod from the aide, but then the woman moved to her left and touched the glass of the cabinet of the alien-like weasel animal, the ten-foot tall beast, and she smiled as she looked up.

On the star map above, the RIM decreased in size, and the visual display moved inward. It moved inward what looked like a large distance, and the world this creature came from was highlighted and enlarged.

"Planet's name, Ma'am, is Peltola, a water world, but it did have small groups of some islands. It lies more than four thousand lights inward, number two in its system, Ma'am ..." she said her voice trailing off.

The Baroness shook her head and stopped herself from looking surprised.

Four thousand lights.

She noted that a red dwarf star, past ten thousand lights away inward, was the sun for this Peltola planet.

Someone had gone from Neres to Peltola to capture this trophy. In pre-Barony Drive time frames, the best speed of the fastest destroyer class ship, with three Tachyon engines, was about 2.5 lights per day; a trip to Peltola would have taken more than four years each way.

The ability to do that was within reach for any baron in the last thousand years since the Tachyon Drive had been invented and rolled out all across the galaxy. But who in the world would sit for more than four years, waiting for a hunt, then hunt, then pack the trophy up, and take four more years to return home? More than eight years on this trip alone—wait.

"How many of these are from inwards, and at what distances, Nancy?"

Nancy referred to the kiosk tablet and then began to hit various onscreen icons. "These, Ma'am, are all more than eight thousand lights," she said, and five cabinets in the grouping lit up within. "These, Ma'am, are all around five thousand lights." More cabinets lit up. "Here's the closest group, all within four or so thousand lights," Nancy said, and the final cabinets lit up.

The Baroness nodded. There were more than forty trophies from as far inward as ten thousand lights. A lot of travel using the Tachyon Drive … and much time spent not here in the Barony, she thought, wondering which baron it might be.

"Wait," she said suddenly, "is there any way to ask the AI who shot these—and how long ago?"

Nancy nodded and pressed some more icons. All the cabinets went dark except for the farthest one at ten thousand lights that held the alien-like weasel.

She clicked one more tablet onscreen, icon and above their heads, beside the display of Peltola, a picture of the hunter showed up, along with dates and even a small group of photos of the hunt.

"That's my husband, the late baron," she said right out loud.

Then she noted the dates.

"And, I do not remember him being away in the eight years we were together—so this cannot be true," she stated emphatically. "In fact, we were on a vacation for almost a month during that time—well, just after it, as I remember," she said.

The dates of the hunt were just before she and the baron had gone to Bottle for a month of downtime, and there was no way he had been gone for eight years at the same time. They'd only been husband and wife for eight years in total.

So… she thought, enough for here and now.

"AI, who am I?" she said. a

The AI chimed once and responded, "Voice certified, you are the Baroness of the Barony."

She nodded. "Then take this down," she said, and she half-smiled at her aide. "I want this part of the palace, in its entirety, sealed off from anyone and everyone else. No one is to have access. I am the only one you will allow to enter this area, and you are to notify me—no matter where I am and what I'm doing—about any kind of access entry

attempt. No exceptions—Baroness code R-88,
please encrypt and seal once we leave."

She turned to her EliteGuards. "You are now
under orders to shoot to kill anyone you find in this
area—other than me—should you need to foist off
an incursion. You," she said to Nancy, "are to tell
no one, and I mean no one, about this area or what
you've found. I want you in my sitting room in
thirty minutes with a full list of every single person
who knows about this. I will decide who will keep
this knowledge—and who will not."

The two EliteGuards snapped to attention and
saluted. Nancy blanched, nodded, and nodded
even more, scared since what had been found had
caused such an issue for her Baroness.

Upon her request, Nancy showed the Baroness
how to control the lights and the kiosk tablet too,
and moments later, the four of them left the trophy
room.

"Access. Is there a secret door somewhere that I
can use rather than the one we entered in?" she
asked.

Nancy nodded. "Yes, Ma'am, there is behind the
flags display in the late baron's private office.
Directly into the trophy room. We came in via what
must have been an alternate escape route—and yes,
Ma'am, I can have it resealed too."

The Baroness nodded and said, "Let's discuss it

later when I get that list," and they all left the area going back the way they had come.

#####

Ambassador Bedre rose to speak to the RIM Confederacy Council, and as he did, he nodded to the aide just behind him. On the huge display panel off to one side of the Council room, a graphic came up of the Duchy d'Avigdor in the form of a star map that was expanded to explain things more easily.

He nodded at the aide and then said in a loud and very polished voice, "My thanks for the opportunity to both attend the Council meeting as the member from the duchy and for the time to make this presentation." He tapped the tablet in front of him.

A large professional photo of the late duke appeared now at the center of the star map over top of the images behind it.

"The duke—David was his name—was a friend. We met in elementary school over almost eighty years ago, and we have remained friends and close for all those decades. He was a man of really simple tastes, and while a true Royal, he was about as fair and tactful as any head of state might ever be. As you all know, he never married. He never, as he used to say, found love in front of him, and for that, he was always slightly apologetic. What that meant was" —the ambassador clicked on his tablet, and a genealogy tree replaced the late duke's face—"that as you can see, there really was no true heir for the duchy."

The tree showed three generations back with only a few branches—all of them ended with no progeny. Even the duke himself, though listed down at the bottom of the family tree, ended with a full stop.

No heirs. No one to take over when he died. No one at all.

"But—and I've learned over the years, when there is a 'but,' there can often be surprise—there is an answer, or rather two answers. that you all do not yet know, and we will speak on both," he said as he hit the tablet screen in front of him once more.

The family tree now disappeared and was replaced with a simple statement that read:

Option Number One: That the Temporary Provisional Government of the Duchy d'Avigdor works over a period of a full year and looks into joining a current RIM Confederacy member realm as a subsidiary of same. The choice of whom to consider, what to offer, and the final deal to be developed will be made by the Temporary Provisional Government at their behest.

He looked around the room and nodded before

going on. "Yes, that would mean that we—and I am the head of that 'Temporary Provisional Government' for the duchy and our six-planet realm—we would put together a short list. We would begin talks with all on that list to eventually reach the best possible deal we can find. And the Duchy d'Avigdor would then fall under that realm's flag."

He smiled, looked down for a second, seemingly to consider what he was going to add, and then went on. "Sitting at this table are the five realms we have already approached—" He held up a hand to stop the stirring around the table.

"We will not reveal who any of those five are—and we still have one more to add to that list. These talks will take months and months for us to 'whittle down' the list to the eventual partner for the Duchy d'Avigdor. We take this very, very seriously, Council members, and it will be a very diligent and deep process ..."

He looked around and the room was spellbound —not a single interruption nor for that matter anyone not paying strict attention.

He smiled once more and clicked the tablet again. The statement on the screen was replaced with a second option that read:

Option Number Two: There is a codicil in the duke's will, that if completed by the person involved, will make Option #1 moot as there will now be a true heir to the Duchy d'Avigdor.

An immediate uproar in the room ensued.

"What kind of guff is that," the Eran head of state barked.

"Who says a will cannot bind a realm," the Madrigal member said dryly.

"I have never heard of this—does that mean there is an heir to the duchy—some kind of a bastard son?" said the Skogg member.

The Skogg member's question stopped all the talk. Even though not a single word was being said, Chairman Gramsci ensured silence remained by banging down two gavels.

"Yes, Ambassador, that does bring up the question. Is there an heir? And if this heir says 'yes,' it appears you mean that the duchy will become led by this person?"

The ambassador just nodded.

"So, is that fully in line with the Duchy d'Avigdor's constitution—and more importantly, have you thought about asking our own RIM Confederacy governance people about this? I should think that you'd want to know up front that what you have outlined as an option would even be legal?"

The ambassador smiled once more and then combed his white hair back off his brow with a hand. "Chairman Gramsci, yes, we have checked with our own duchy constitutional experts and with other experts on both wills and trusts and such codicils too. All have agreed that this course of action by the late duke is both legal and may be followed by us, the Temporary Provisional Government, too."

The Baroness leaned forward. "And, do you have a favorite, Ambassador—Option Number One or Option Number Two?"

The ambassador realized this was a loaded question as the five realms that were a part of Option Number One were in front of him, so he just shrugged. "Ma'am, we are following the late duke's will, and I do not have the right to have a favorite. We will proceed with both of them, and eventually, one will rise to fruition, Ma'am."

She nodded back to him and leaned back in her chair.

The ambassador wondered if she was satisfied with his answer, but he knew that after more than five decades in the Duchy Diplomatic Corps, he could lie so convincingly that he believed it himself.

The chairman looked around the room. "Do we have any more questions on the duchy presentation," he inquired.

Not a word was said, and he sighed and tossed both gavels down onto the table in front of him.

"Then I'll ask it. Who is the heir—or perhaps, the potential heir—Ambassador?"

The ambassador grinned, looked around the room at all the faces that were pointed to him, and spoke quietly. "I am not at liberty to say, but I can tell you, the late duke held this person in the highest regard ..." He sat, turning off the display panel, and once again, the room was silent.

As he looked around the room, he could see wheels spinning in brains as they all wondered who the heir might be and what their relationship might be with this unknown new duke.

The Baroness, who was on the Option Number One list, was lost in thought, which he found highly amusing, as the potential heir was her new son-in-law.

The Caliph, also on that list, played with a stylo on his tablet, tapping the point over and over against the screen.

The Prince of Thrones, also on the list, smiled at him directly and tipped his head to one side as if to say "Nice presentation, Ambassador." At least that's what the ambassador thought it might have meant.

The Earl of Merilda wouldn't even look at him, and though they too were on the Option Number One list, the ambassador had had some misgivings on that proposed amalgamation too.

The head of state for Hope and its three-world realm was absent today, so he had no way to gauge what his Option Number Two surprise might mean to them. But one thing was for sure; they'd know quickly as Ansibles must be ringing all over the RIM with the news and guesses of who the potential heir was.

The final member of that list, so far not even approached, was Genie and the Djan; their leader was in the dark. That name just added to the list had come after months of discussions and research and arguments both for and against. Genie was a realm that was both human and alien, which had been something of a sticking point, but it had finally been decided that Genie was to be approached and asked to start talks too.

He didn't bother to listen to the clerk who had risen to announce Agenda item number five. He leaned forward to work on his tablet to send Lord Scott an EYES ONLY. He wanted to let the man know that his presentation had just been made to the RIM Confederacy Council. They were now aware that an unknown potential heir was out in the open, but his identity had been kept a secret. He gave Lord Scott a gentle reminder that he had only about eleven months to make up his mind, do his due diligence, so to speak. He attached the short list of the Option Number One list of other realms for

Lord Scott's attention and reminded him that if he chose to follow the duke's codicil, this would supersede the other realms and Lord Scott would become Duke Scott d'Avigdor ...

#####

Tanner leaned forward and spoke directly at Admiral McQueen, his forefinger stabbing down at the desk with each sentence.

"Admiral, yes, I do understand, but you too must see that the RIM Navy can offer little for the admiral to do. Now that the whole new Eons Naval Academy is built, up and running, and done. Higgins was, without a doubt, the best call you've ever made—but, Sir, to find him something else to do now is going to be a hard found goal," he said as his finger stopped in midair.

Admiral McQueen leaned back to noodle that around for a moment and then a moment more.

Tanner knew his argument had made sense. The RIM Confederacy Navy, while small with less than thirty ships, had more admirals than there were real needs for—at least in his mind. Admiral Higgins had nowhere to go, really. The building of the new naval academy was over, and now the man was sitting in his office in Navy Hall on Juno. With nothing to do.

McQueen leaned back over toward the console in

the EYES ONLY Ansible call and half-smiled. "I cannot order Admiral Higgins to resign, but what I might be able to do is to talk to him, gauge his interest, and perhaps talk him into a, say, two-year posting with the Barony Navy. He'd still be on our payroll though. Would that work for you, Lord Scott?" he asked.

Tanner shook his head. "Sorry, Admiral, but not a workable solution. We want a real live admiral—one who's on our payroll and therefore owes us his allegiance. I would suggest that he be perhaps allowed to take a pro-tem retirement—and then join us. Later, say, in those couple of years, he can decide. We need him, Admiral, and in my world, there's only one better candidate who I doubt would even countenance a move," he said pointedly.

McQueen nodded, his face a mask. "I hear you, Lord Scott, and I can say, under those conditions, yes, you have my permission to talk to Admiral Higgins. I hope he asks some really tough questions, but I'm also wise enough to know that you have a great candidate—one who will make the Barony Navy proud," he finished off.

He hadn't acknowledged that other candidate that Tanner had mentioned, as he well knew he was number one. But he'd never leave the RIM Confederacy Navy.

Tanner spoke up last. "And, Admiral, I see the fourth star has been added to your collar—well done, Sir!" he said as he acknowledged the new rank of full admiral that McQueen had just been given. He, of course, had known for months now that the fourth star was on its way, but it was good to see it in the flesh.

That did get a bit of a flush on the admiral's cheeks, and he nodded and signed off.

Tanner turned and looked out the Barony Palace windows down at the gardens below. Here, in the new wing of the palace, the palace gardeners still handled the landscaping. Below, in the space where his wedding ceremony had taken place just a few months back, was a huge plain grass field. Around the outside of same was a low, white wall of stones he'd heard were imported from Carnarvon. White was what he'd call them from way up here on the third floor of the residential wing, but he knew that as one got closer, there was a red snake of crystals that ran in every stone. At sunset, he'd often made it a point to look out to see how the stones shone in the dusky sky, as the orange sunlight caught the exact crystal glowing brightly.

At the close end of that field, he could see only the top of the small monument that had been placed at the same location as the wedding ceremony altar had been located. The same Carnarvon marbles were the walkway around the single monolithic block of the same marble, and it had nothing carved on it. There had been, he'd heard later, some talk of what to write and whom to list on the block—so it had been left as a simple large block of the marble.

He stared down at the gardener closest to him who was cutting the short hedge around the block of marble, and he wondered if the area was ever visited by Barony citizens. He'd have to ask.

That question was added to his mental list and replaced the question about the candidate for the new admiral's job. He'd already made that call to Ethan directly just a few hours ago, and he'd gotten the sense the man was really without purpose. He'd asked him in a circuitous way if he'd entertain a new adventure, which had perked up the man's ears, and Ethan had grinned and said yes in a hundred ways, without ever vocalizing he was out of sorts with the RIM Navy.

He'd not told McQueen and that he wasn't proud of. He certainly should have—but he had to know that the candidate would entertain a change before he could ask his mentor, Admiral McQueen, for the leeway to do that. Shouldn't be hard to hide that fact, and he grinned as he was watching that gardener.

The man had a problem with a patch of the hedge, which it seemed he just couldn't get to look right, and he stepped back to peer down the long hedge. In front of him, it dipped a bit lower than the areas he'd already cut. He somehow had not been able to keep the top of his trimming on an even keel. While not being a gardener, Tanner thought there was only one way to fix that now—go back and trim the area behind him down to the new level; almost a hundred yards of hedge would need to be redone.

The gardener, however, was not new to his business, and he dropped his laser trimmer onto the turf at his feet, reached into an unseen box of tools, and came up with what looked like some other kind of laser tool. He bent over and then knelt down at the low spot in front of him. Tanner could see him reaching into the thick hedge foliage with that tool. As he watched, Tanner edged up a bit on his chair to have a better view, and as he did that, the hedge in front of the man was slowly getting a bit taller. "Some tool," Tanner said to himself, "but I wonder how you'd get branches and stems to lengthen like that with a laser—or some kind of a tool. Must ask."

He wondered if all Royals did this. And he shrugged. Hardly. He had the curiosity of a naval captain—and even now as Lord Scott, he still couldn't get rid of that characteristic of himself.

Higgins was in. He had a new Barony Navy fleet

admiral, and that made him happy. What that might bring would be more than interesting, but as a Royal, he knew he'd supersede all.

#####

As Ambassador Adam Bedre walked down the final few feet of the long hallway in the ducal palace, he wondered for a second or two, as he always did at this point, what the hell the designer had thought as he'd laid out the plans for this area. Where the public areas of the palace met the residential area should be a very noticeable change, he believed. Doing so would prevent any kind of issues of misunderstanding of where anyone was headed. It would keep the residential area, where the duke lived, private and under wraps, so to speak.

Yet as he walked on the black-and-white tiles, the heels of his boots clicking on the tiles, the next step would see those tiles change to black and red, but other than that, there was no noticeable change to the hallway. Yet this was a residential hallway now and ahead of him was the only door to the residential area.

He went right up to the door and laid a palm on the security plate on the doorframe. The door clicked twice as the palace AI recognized him as a person who had access to the residential area, and the door opened on its own.

He was the only one on Neen who could access this residential area now as it'd been closed off from all other personnel at the death of the duke. He, of course, with his long past as a true friend of the duke's, was not counted as having access officially either, which was another good thing.

He sighed. He'd been granted that access more than fifty years ago, when he'd been the duke's college roommate and had been able to enter any area of the palace after that status had been verified. He'd been close to the duke. David had never lost his sense of self and had proven himself to be a good leader. They had gone from college roommates to close friends, and that friendship had been the best thing in both of their lives. He grinned as he went through the door and down the red-and-black tiled hallway toward the study. The duke had called this room the study, where he kept his office and ran the duchy from, and everyone else had followed suit.

Adam smiled once more, remembering the time when he and David had been totally drunk, and both had thrown up right here on the door-sill of the study, and then David had asked for a steward to clean up same. Little did he know that the palace AI had reported all to David's father—the duke at the time —and he'd paid for that.

Crossing that sill, he stepped quickly over to the desk, sat on the chair behind it, and leaned back. This was David's most inner sanctum—where he had run the duchy from—and he knew that just by sitting in the chair he'd—

He let the tears come. His best friend had been killed—murdered by an assassin—the sister of the one the duke wanted to make his heir.

"Over my dead body," he said to himself once yet again, and the tears slowly subsided.

David had made only that one single mistake in his whole life—the codicil that offered the dukedom and the duchy to Lord Scott. And it was his job to make sure that never happened.

He knew he had little chance—even as the head of the Temporary Provisional Government—to challenge that codicil. So he had planned to make the opportunity less of same by getting the short list of suitors down to one great choice.

He didn't actually care for the Caliphate—and yet the Barony was only a bit of a better choice. The Baroness was the issue, he thought, as he wiped away the tear tracks and cleared his throat. He looked down at the desktop and the list itself—now with only two names on it. He wondered what else he might do to somehow sully the Caliphate a notch or two. Not enough to ever show that he had anything to do with it, but enough for the rest of the provisional committee to look at and to slightly curl up a lip. Enough to make the Barony just slightly better. It had to be enough—but only enough—to appear as the simplest reason to choose the Barony.

He looked over, past the chairs on the other side of the desk, to the large bookcase in front of him. There were sections that the duke had had salted with items from all over the duchy. Each of the six planets was there, from Neen to Anulet, and each was cluttered with knickknacks and tchotchkes. He'd picked up and looked at some of them earlier, but now he just stared at them.

He needed to tarnish—yes, that word suited his quest—tarnish the Caliphate, but how?

On the RIM, the Caliphate was what one might call the "armpit" of realms: gambling; women of all species, humans and aliens; extortion too, it was said; smuggling; and yes, even murder too. How to paint that realm as a non-player in taking over the duchy was going to be an interesting point to try to make.

He sat and toyed with the list as he wondered how one could tarnish what was already tarnished.

CHAPTER FOUR

The beauty of the room struck him immediately once more. Tanner settled in to the deep leather wingback chair in an area labeled as the VIP room, by the bailiff who'd showed them in. Courtrooms, he'd heard, were always built to impress the innocent ... the guilty just didn't care. Out before him, beyond the one-way glass wall in front, lay massive pieces of furniture carved from what looked like dark mahogany. Wall hangings, drapes, and Barony flags were behind the three judges' dais. Their chairs were tall and covered with blue leather. Even the bench in the prisoner's box was the same dignified blue, but in velvet, as he remembered when he'd sat on same long ago. The floor was covered with a scarlet red carpet, and off to his right, in the public area, were a few people as visitors.

He looked over at Helena and smiled, and she squeezed his hand.

"Honey, you're going to be okay, right?" she queried, and he could tell she was worried about him

Why would that be? In moments, my sister, Gia, the assassin who had killed both the Master Adept and my friend the duke would be led in for her first appearance in court. What about that would cause me anguish?

"They said the whole area we're behind is one-way glass we can see out of, but everyone in the courtroom cannot see through. We got spirited in by our EliteGuards, and no one knows—Gia will not know—that you are here, love," she said, still squeezing his hand.

He attempted to smile at her and nodded. Beyond the glass wall, off to one side, the bailiff who had escorted him into the courtroom led in the prisoner.

Gia looked fit, he thought.

She was shackled, but still each step was measured, and she seemed to bounce along behind the bailiff until he seated her on the blue velvet banquette and attached her wrist cuffs to the stanchion beside her.

Her hair needed some cutting, some makeup

perhaps, and better, more court-impressive clothes, Tanner thought as he went through a list of what would help her look her best—and he stopped himself cold at that thought. I am here to watch her take her medicine—not to help in any way.

The bailiff then barked out loudly, "Order, order ... order in the court," and the talking stopped immediately. Directly in front of Tanner, at what would be the prosecutor's desk, a man rose to speak to the court.

"I am told that this is a continuance, Your Honors, for the accused, one Gia Scott. Without going over any of the evidence against her, which includes video—professional quality video—of her shooting—"

"Objection, Your Honors," the defense attorney said as he jumped up to his feet. "The prosecution cannot present any evidence at this time, or, for that matter, these fraudulent videos which we will move to strike them all at the proper time, Your Honors," the young man said, leaning forward toward the bench where the three judges sat.

Wonder who picked out this guy, Tanner thought, and he made a mental note to check on that later.

The judges didn't even confer on his objection, and the one in the middle said quite dryly, "Objection sustained. Mr. Prosecutor, you know better than that—and further, that is all for the accused's actual trial. This is a continuance hearing, and so we'd ask that you please stick to that item only."

The prosecutor didn't even flinch, Tanner noticed, wondering why he'd even bothered to say that about the video. The man obviously realized that was for another time.

Everyone knew Gia had killed those two at his wedding, and, yes, there were dozens of very professional videos shot of the actual event, which included her using the camera that held a gun to shoot and kill two of Tanner's friends.

The prosecutor said, "My apologies to the court. Our continuance today is to ask that the accused be remanded over to the Barony Hospital Ship for full mental and psychiatric testing.

Sanity is a legal term denoting that an individual is of sound mind and therefore can bear legal responsibility for his or her actions. The official legal term is compos mentis. It is generally defined in terms of the absence of insanity—non compos mentis. It is not a medical term, although the opinions of medical experts are often important in making a legal decision as to whether someone is sane or insane. And we ask for no time frame for this part of her sentence."

He stopped for a moment to look down at a

paper in front of him. "We therefore petition the court that to establish whether or not the accused, Gia Scott, is sane would be the first logical step in her trial. If found sane, she will stand trial as charged for murder. If found insane, she will remain up on the Hospital Ship in their secure psychiatric ward until such time as she is found sane, Your Honors."

Once again, Gia's defense counsel jumped to his feet. "Your Honors well know that those acquitted of a federal offense by reason of insanity have not been able to challenge their psychiatric confinement through a writ of habeas corpus or other remedies.

"We hereby serve notice that without such a trial, we need to place a limit—Your Honors need to place a limit—on this sanity evaluation time to be spent by my client up on the Hospital Ship. They could keep her there indefinitely without any way for us to gain her freedom, Your Honors. Surely that is not what such an observation and analysis should be for," he said.

The defense counsel took a deep breath and continued forcefully. "She is not guilty of anything at this point, Your Honors, so such a continuance sentence amounts to unfair and unconstitutional imprisonment on the Hospital Ship with no time limits instated at all."

The judges conferred on that one, Tanner noted.

That young attorney had made some sense of this.

Putting Gia in the psychiatric ward for evaluation for years and years was really circumventing the whole "innocent until proven guilty" axiom.

This guy was good, Tanner thought, or at least he was young enough to not fear the Barony and its powers over his career.

The middle judge nodded and said, "We hereby grant the petition of the accused to be remanded up to the Barony Hospital Ship for up to one full year for full observation, monitoring, and analysis. Reports to be tendered back to the court for sanity hearing at that time, on a monthly basis. In one year, she is to be released back to the courts for trial no matter what the findings are. Until then, for this case, we are adjourned ..."

Tanner stirred and looked over at Helena.

"It was me," she said. "I found this young man— one Jordan Alpert—after bothering to read some reports from our judicial minister on how the young man was able to get some 'carved in stone' cases un-carved! I figured that as she is your sister, she deserves the best attorney we could find.

"Took a few weeks of careful planning while we were on Bottle—you thought I had that real need for all those Reiki stone massages about a month or so ago ... not true. I was on Ansible with staff arranging for him to be hired to be your sister's attorney. Hidden, mind you, behind a storefront legal shop in Neres City. No one will ever trace it back to me—to us, I guess I mean—honey," she said sheepishly.

He looked at her and smiled. "Figures that my wife would be ahead of me—part of being married," he said and leaned forward to kiss her.

As he straightened out, he looked across the courtroom to see the bailiff was undoing Gia's cuffs from the stanchion beside her. She stood, looking almost straight at him.

Helena noted that too. "She can't see us, Tanner," she said.

"But she might believe that I'm right here," he said.

Gia. Gia, what have you done ... he thought as he and Helena rose to go back to the palace.

On the Neres Navy base, Tanner was being taken for a tour with his aide, Lieutenant Kiraz, and they'd only now gotten to the new building.

"Lieutenant, there was a time-line for this one, right?" he asked, and she nodded as she looked down at her tablet to search for that date.

Already today, he'd seen the latest incarnation of the Captains Council chambers up on the second floor of the current administration building, and it had passed, he'd thought, with flying colors. It was perfectly laid out and, as his aide had known, ready for the upcoming new captains for the new Barony Navy ships. She'd thought of just about everything, and he wondered just how he'd not thought of that. But that's what aides are for, we Royals claim.

That made him grin and he turned his head to one side, so Ayla wouldn't see it.

In an even tone, she said, "Sir, says here that the first date for occupancy permits to be issued was a month ago."

He grunted and looked at the enormous concrete piers and foundation pillars that were still wet and shiny. The building—at least as far as he could tell—was still months away from completion. The deadline had obviously been missed, and as he was about to ask her for more details, the sound of a ship coming in drowned out any conversation for a minute or two.

It was a RIM Navy vessel—the RN Rigel, and his next meeting with his new admiral was on same. He shaded his brow with a hand and watched as the pilot dropped her down perfectly, which for a six-hundred-foot cruiser was not an easy task, right onto her landing pad. As the dusts quickly diminished, he could see the usual greeting party of Customs and Health officers heading out on their small vehicles. As expected, the landing ramp came down quickly thereafter.

He smiled. "Admiral Higgins is going to be early. I like folks who are early in all things, I think," he said.

His aide nodded. "Sir, I might offer that the completion of this new naval admin building might be a great first project for the new admiral?" she casually offered, and he knew he'd picked well when he'd chosen her.

"My thoughts exactly, Lieutenant. And as my aide, you do realize that you're going to be the one who will 'liaise' between Higgins and me—right?" he asked.

She nodded once more. "Aye, Sir. And he'll get the same speedy help I always offer. I would think that there will be tons of that help needed starting today—but that it will slowly fade as he finds his way," she said as she reached in her pocket and handed Tanner a small black box.

For a Hopian, she was taller than most, but she carried it well. Knowing that you want to excel in the navy—any realm's navy—meant that you had to follow the normal rules. Work hard and long; exercise to keep a more than healthy body; take professional development courses; and participate in extracurricular activities, often seeking the opportunities out.

Ayla was at the top of her game, and Tanner was

sure she'd excel. Her smile was the best feature she had. She was pretty enough with that tinge of red in her auburn hair, and she did, he'd admit, look great in her uniform. And considering that Hope was her home world, which was known as a really hardworking human realm, it further meant that she would excel. He knew that and it was partly up to him to help by both being a hard-nosed Royal as well as a mentor.

He nodded back to her as they both turned to face the Jeep as it was pulling up in front of them.

Admiral Higgins disembarked from the Jeep, strode up to face them, and smiled as he came to full attention and saluted.

Tanner smiled back, offered a return salute, and then stepped forward to offer his hand. "Welcome, Admiral. We are all so pleased that you've accepted our offer to become the new head of the Barony Navy—and these are for you," he finished off as he handed the man the small black box.

Higgins had a quizzical look on his face. He opened the box, took one look at its contents, and then snapped it shut. "Lord Scott, I am more than surprised by the honor. I imagined that—as the new navy admiral to replace yourself—I'd be a single-star admiral. But this box, Sir, contains five stars, which would make me a fleet admiral, Sir. Do I have that right?" he asked, his voice solemn and reverent.

Tanner nodded. "Aye, Admiral. Fleet admiral for the Barony Navy—in fact, for all of the Barony Forces—is what you are as of today, Sir. Get your steward to order full new uniforms for same, and enjoy the rank. Trust me, there are going to be days when you think it's all not worth it—at least there were for me, Admiral. And welcome aboard, Ethan!" he finished off.

Higgins grinned at him, tucked the black box into a pocket, and then looked around them. "Construction coming along, is it?" he asked.

Tanner glanced at his aide and nodded.

"Sir, yes, 'along' might be a word that would apply," Ayla said. "However, it's already a full month past the final dates for occupancy permits to be applied for ..." she finished, her voice trailing off.

Higgins tilted his head, and a hint of a smile crossed his lips. "Then I'd guess I want to see files on same—may I ask, Lord Scott, if I can instruct your aide to get me same? Or do I need to go through other channels—sorry to have to ask about this so soon, but I've got the stars. Time to earn them," he said.

Tanner grinned at him. "Admiral, Lieutenant Kiraz is my real strength—and yes, as she's in the navy, she technically works for you, so command away," he said.

Higgins smiled and gestured with his head. He and the lieutenant ambled away from him and began to talk among themselves.

Tanner looked back at the Rigel and noted she was getting outfitted by the base chandlers. A group of sailors was leaving the ship on what looked like shore leave duty. He thought back to his days of getting his land legs back for shore leave and enjoying new planets and the local cultures. He's thought there was nothing better than to have a beer or a scotch and just sit and soak up a new culture. He'd done it all over the RIM and the Earldom inward, and he knew how important shore leave was for a crewman.

The new admiral and his aide were lost in conversation while she showed him something on his tablet. Tanner walked toward the Rigel, and in a few short minutes, he was just behind a CWO on the tarmac who was having some troubles with a chandler over supplies.

"Yes, but as I said, and as our requisition says, we want complete cables—not ones like these that still need splicing and then for the RJ45 connectors to be installed and then tested. With over two hundred of these cables, we don't have the time to do that— which is why we req'd 'complete' cables," he said, his voice exasperatedly tight.

The chandler looked down at the requisition in his hands and then back at the CWO, and he shrugged his shoulders. "Then maybe you should'a ordered them way before pulling in—it'd take, what, three days for one of our staff to complete these two hundred cables. And you ordered them just yesterday," he said, crossing his arms.

From what Tanner could see, the chandler did have a point. "Might I inquire—"

Realizing a Royal stood behind them, the two men jumped to attention after the usual half-bow one gave a Royal.

"Why the sudden order for same?" Tanner finished.

"Don't really know, Lord Scott," the CWO said, his eyes locked on the horizon as he answered as best he could as he went on. "We were just told yesterday to pick these up and get them to Ghayth immediately. Came right from Commander Williams' offices, Lord Scott," he answered, his voice only barely audible now.

Tanner nodded. "Then might I offer that you get some men on this STAT, Chief Warrant Officer? Commander Williams will want them at about the same speed, I'd imagine. Chandler, thank you for your help so far on this," he said, and he walked away.

Royals shouldn't interfere in the little things, he'd

been told by Helena time and time again. So next time, he'd have to see if he could just ignore the little things. He walked across the tarmac toward Admiral Higgins and Lieutenant Kiraz, who were still deep in conversation. He wondered why Williams and Ghayth would need more WAN cables, as that made almost no sense to him.

"Fodder for another day," he said to himself. "A Royal's life was so hard ... wasn't it?"

#####

She wondered who had originally designed the bridge—in fact, all spaceship bridges—as she once again tried to get comfortable in the huge, well-padded leather "Royals" chair on the bridge of the *Atlas*, and while she had the answer, it just wouldn't do.

The Seenra, the builder race for most ships, was just one culprit, she knew. But while they built the ships, it was the specifications sent to builders, which included the arrangement of each of the consoles and tiers of seating on a bridge, she wanted to know more about.

She once again rose, folded up her right leg this time, and then dropped back onto the seat to squirm to find a more comfortable position. She leaned a bit to her left and then tucked her bare foot up higher below her left thigh to try to ease how uncomfortable she felt. But it was no use.

I am going to be antsy, she thought, and that is it. Thank God, the Barony Drive meant that instead of it being weeks between Neres and Ghayth, it was now seconds. She nodded to the *Atlas* captain and said, "Proceed, Captain."

The star in the target center of the huge view-screen of the ship was suddenly solid as the *Atlas* went into the Barony Drive. As she watched, that star grew greatly in only a few seconds.

Captain Hauling smiled and nodded as the helmsman stated the obvious.

"Sir, we are now off Ghayth, in low orbit, and the trip took ... only eight seconds, Sir," he said.

Hauling looked over at her. "Ma'am, will you be going down to meet with the commander or ..."

Her brows furrowed as she thought on that, and then she nodded to herself. "Captain, I will need a shuttle to take me down to meet with him, please arrange for that in, say, one hour."

She rose from her seat and tucked her radiantly green toes in the open-faced sandals she'd kicked off earlier. She slowly made her way off the bridge and back to her quarters down on Deck Forty-nine, just down one from the bridge. Once she went through her doors, she once again kicked off those sandals and barked at her quarter's AI. "Find me a steward, AI, STAT."

In less than a minute, as she was just settling into the loveseat she so favored in the sitting room area, a man asked nicely what he could get for her.

"Wine—something on the specialty list, please, a nice red," she answered.

Her sommelier had set up her favorites in lists, so she could just ask for something on a list and not have to bother trying to remember a wine's name or vintage. Being a Royal was such a difficult job.

She said, "AI, show me Ghayth, please, full color."

In front of her, the whole exterior bulkhead suddenly dissolved as the planet popped up on the display. Gray. Ghayth was gray; there was no doubt about that, as the continents she could see were just that. Oceans, however, were blue, underneath much less cloud cover, and there appeared to be a storm in the southern hemisphere as she could see the circular formations of a hurricane.

"Wouldn't want to be out on a boat in that," she said to herself and then snorted.

With no sentient life, no one was out on a boat, and yet she still knew that storms that big caused much more than a ripple of misfortune.

She stopped cold in her thinking. She had been looking for a way to get the Duchy d'Avigdor to consider her Barony to be their natural successor.

She was on their list, but so were others.

To get the Duchy d'Avigdor by "hook or by crook," as her father used to say, was fair game. However, she'd not yet found a way to circumvent the list process and simply take over the six-planet realm.

The storm below offered her an answer to gain that type of an advantage, and she smiled as she connived. An event would need to happen to threaten the duchy.

She—the Barony, she meant—would need to save the Duchy d'Avigdor by taking them over to quell the threat. And she would then own same.

It wasn't perfect, but it was the start to formulating a plan; by following the final plan, she would gain six new planets for her Barony—and then the chairmanship of the RIM Confederacy Council.

As the clouds roiled in their circular clockwise paths, she thought she could see the rain bands around the eye. She wondered just how violent it was, but she didn't bother to ask the AI for details.

Instead, she thought about what kind of storm she could create that would suck up the duchy and allow the Barony to offer aid—and win the day.

What kind of a storm could I create is the question …

#####

Prime Minister Kondo Lazaro moved gracefully from the red and blue Jeep and onto the driveway in front of the Barony Palace. He'd been home on Amasis just two hours ago and had flown in on the frigate the BN Jericho; it had taken longer to get a Jeep and get over here to the palace than it had to come the seven lights from his own planet to Neres.

"Such a short ride meant he'd not had the chance to get his "space legs" on—nor for that matter to get back to gravity either," he said to himself, and he snorted at his not being a real navy man anymore.

His boots crunched on the shoulders of the huge circular driveway as he strode up the giant walkway to the steps that led to the enormous double doors to the palace. He'd been here a few times before, when he'd been in the Barony Navy, and he'd learned early and well that it was best to play dumb to everyone in the palace—except the Baroness.

His meeting today was with her, and he was a bit un-nerved as he'd not been able to figure out what was the agenda of today's meeting—nor was he able to prepare for same.

Un-nerved. Yes, that about said it, and he climbed the large, wide steps and presented himself at the EliteGuard station at the door.

"I am—"

"Mr. Prime Minister, we know you, Sir, and we acknowledge that you are here to see the Baroness. Please follow the lieutenant who will guide you to the meeting room, Sir," the EliteGuard at the doorway said, and he smiled nicely as he dipped his head in recognition for the visitor's position as a head of state.

Nicely done, Kondo thought, and he smiled. With that kind of greeting, one might think what would follow would be just as nice. He hoped he was right.

The EliteGuard lieutenant spun on his heels and walked toward the huge doorway that the palace AI opened for them. Inside, as Kondo followed along, they went through room after room with furniture and aesthetics more posh than he'd remembered. One room, he knew as soon as he entered, but he slowed down as they entered. The center of the large, long room was filled with a beautiful round table that must have been forty feet across. At the very center of that table—maybe made of wood from Gayaza—lay a vase that must have been twenty feet tall. But now, he saw, instead of sitting at the exact center of the table, it hung in midair, about three feet up off the table.

He paused as he was following the lieutenant and pointed. "Lieutenant, any idea on how that vase is floating off the table?"

The EliteGuard shrugged. "Not a clue—Barony secrets I'd guess, Sir," he said, and he spun once more and led the way across the rest of the long room, and Kondo followed.

They moved through three more large rooms and a corridor that had no art on the walls but on the floor instead. He'd thought he was supposed to walk around the paintings below his feet, but instead he just did what the lieutenant did and stepped along normally.

In what must have been the meeting room, he was pointed to a small setting of facing loveseats and took a spot on one. As he looked around, he saw immediately that he was not alone. Across from him on the arm of that loveseat, an animal—a pet of some kind—was staring at him.

He stared back.

It was a tawny brown with patches of iridescent blue—and it had fur. Sort of. When the animal—he decided he was going to call it a cat—breathed, the brown and iridescent blue waved like fur. It had what looked like three ears placed around its head like a tiara, and they were blue too. He could see four legs and a tail that was as long as the medium-sized cat.

Its eyes did not blink, and he blinked quickly to try to catch the cat blinking—but it just did not blink.

Its eyes were the same shade of blue but brighter. Just staring at him.

He wondered for a moment about poisonous bites, the claws on those paws, and more, but it just looked at him.

He hadn't even noticed, but from his right, the Baroness had appeared. She scooped up her cat and sat heavily on the opposing loveseat.

She was in blue too, but not the same shade. Instead, she was dressed in a bird's egg blue with a dusting of gold he could barely see until it twinkled as it gathered ambient light from the room.

She nodded at someone behind him, and she said, "Please, the same Quaran white as at lunch," and she waved the steward away even though Kondo had never seen the servant.

Moments later, a glass appeared on the table in front of him as the steward returned, served the two glasses of wine, and then disappeared again.

She picked up the cat and placed it on the seat beside her, and it stretched as it rose up onto all fours. Hopping down off the loveseat, it walked off, but he was surprised to see it walk with such an odd gait. Instead of walking like a cat, one leg in front of the other, it moved one leg over the top of the same leg on the other side and moved sideways. The two left legs reached over the two right legs, and then putting them down, it picked up the right legs and moved them over to the right.

Sideways. The cat walked sideways. He shook his head.

The Baroness said a bit dryly, "If you think its gait looks odd here in the sitting room, you should see it hunting prey on Anulet."

He smiled. Interesting animal ...

She smiled at him. "Prime Minister Lazaro, I am glad that you could find the time to meet with me today," she said.

He nodded to her and ensured his head dipped in the traditional bow to a Royal too. "Ma'am, the quickness of travel now on the RIM due to the release of the Barony Drive has made it very easy," he said and smiled once more.

She nodded and waved away the compliment. "I have asked you here today, Kondo," she said with a familiarity that could only come from a Royal, "so that we can discuss an upcoming issue. An issue of great importance to the Barony, which means it is of similar importance to Amasis too."

He sat and listened for more than an hour as she queried his loyalty to the Barony and to Amasis as well. Once satisfied, she spelled out how she was determined to gain the Duchy d'Avigdor and merge it with the Barony. Finally, she spoke about how he might help—if he would consider same.

For many minutes after that, Kondo asked

several questions, and eventually he nodded. He
didn't like what he'd heard, but he knew in his
heart of hearts that it would be for the best—and
would trump all the other powers here in the RIM
Confederacy too.

In the end, he agreed. The planet of Amasis was
in, and as its head of state, he had a large part to
play.

His part might mean the difference between
success and failure for the realm, as well as a new
role for him too.

CHAPTER FIVE

A typical academic, Tanner thought as he nodded and listened to Professor Randall Reynolds as he gave the xeno team leaders' report in person.

He'd flown in on the *Sword,* and it had taken less than a full minute to travel from Neres to Ghayth. Tanner had spent more time walking across the enormous new landing tarmac on Base-1 and had been met by Commander Williams in person. Nice to see, Tanner thought, that simply being a Royal meant you got the most polite, politically correct treatment from all the citizens here on the RIM. At least so far.

Williams had greeted him nicely and had walked with Tanner since he'd wanted to walk to the administration building and forgo riding in the Jeep, which followed behind them.

"Lord Scott, so nice to have you here, and might I say that we were all so happy with your full recovery as well," Williams said.

"Thank you, Commander. Base-1 looks like she's growing pretty quickly too. We're going to have to give the city a real name soon …"

Many cranes topped the city outside the far base walls as new buildings were going up against the gray skyline. What had been a simple plain running down to the ocean was now a city with more than two hundred thousand new citizens. All the citizens of Base-1 had taken the pioneer option offered by the Barony to its citizens across the realm. Move to Ghayth and receive government funds for your new home, or farm with free land, or start a business—it mattered not what you wanted. Ghayth would accommodate the citizens' needs. Most realms established the pioneer option setup for their newest planets after acquisition had occurred.

He walked and made what he now called "Royal-chat" with the commander, careful to nod a lot and say well done often, but there was no real substance to the conversation. Updates on the latest population and demographics figures might have been important to someone else, but for me, Tanner thought, it's just yadda, yadda, yadda.

He allowed the commander to open up the

administration door after the ten-minute walk, and while the planet was gray and misty, as always, he did enjoy the short walk. Inside, a lieutenant led Tanner up a flight of stairs to the second floor and then down a long hallway to the conference room.

He paused at the doorway and realized the whole xeno team had been assembled to meet with him, but the only one actually seated at the table was Professor Randall Reynolds. The rest sat behind him on the far side of the table against the wall, and all rose when he walked into the room.

Royalty again.

He smiled at them and then went to take the chair at the head of the table—Helena had drummed that into him. Royalty commands from the power chair, she had said to him, so take that chair. And if there was not one, make one. So far, he'd had it pretty easy, and he lowered himself into the business chair and pulled himself closer to the table.

"Be seated, please, one and all," he said.

Everyone sat at once. Commander Williams took the seat on Tanner's right and the xeno team leader sat on his left. Commander Williams introduced the professor, and he and the rest then waited for the xeno team leader to begin.

It had taken almost an hour for the man to make his presentation. Sometimes, he'd had the video display show items, like the huge arctic warehouse they had discovered. There were more videos about how the door to the bridge of the wrecked ship could teleport items to that warehouse too.

There were also still images detailing the floor plans of the ship, breakdowns of the bridge areas and the consoles, labeled rooms, and inventory lists. Close-up photos of alien technology, including the alien step-plates that allowed a winged alien to stand in midair without hovering by using their wings, took up several minutes of the meeting.

The report was quite detailed. All xeno team groups had contributed. Linguistics had the least amount of information; however, they too appeared to be making some progress.

"Our aliens," Reynolds said finally, "were more advanced than us for sure, yet we're making headway in the first steps of finding those differences. As we work on learning the how-tos of those items, i.e., for care and control of the functionality of them, it's a much slower process— but so far, so good, Lord Scott," he said, and he looked like he'd finished.

Tanner would have liked to have taken notes, but he'd been schooled that taking notes was one more thing a Royal never did themselves. If he wanted, he could just ask that the report be sent to his aide, Ayla. He wondered for a moment if he should have brought her along, but then he thought not for something like this.

He nodded and looked over at Commander Williams. "Commander, no issues at all with security around the wreck, I take it?" he asked

Williams shook his head. "Not at all, Sir. We have marines under Major Stal there, and he tells me that it's not as yet even a hint of a rumor here on Ghayth. He sends his regards, too, Lord Scott, but was unable to make it here today as he's on Amasis for the afternoon but will return for evening chow — er, dinner—Lord Scott. We would very much like to have you stay for that meal. Stal and the professor will be there, and we can chat a bit more on this wreck too, if you'd consider same?"

Tanner looked away for a moment and then back at the commander. "Would love to stay, Commander. Just let me know what time. I'm going to pop down to look over the wreck itself this afternoon as well, but I will return for that dinner then too.

"Professor, 'til then—and please thank your team for their work and efforts. I know we will learn all there is to learn with your team at the helm," he said and smiled.

He knew that if he'd been a plain navy captain, he'd have had several more questions about their findings, but Royals, he reminded himself, delegated those chores to others. He needed his aide, Ayla, and he made a mental note to include her much more often. He would return to the *Sword* and send off a request for her to come to Ghayth this afternoon. She could then join him, and he'd bring her back tomorrow.

As he rose, and the rest of the room did likewise, he was about to say he'd need quarters for the evening, but then he realized that was exactly the kind of thing that an aide—an aide that was present perhaps—would be in charge of.

He smiled as he went over to shake the professor's hand. The man beamed back at him and just about fell all over himself with plans for his trip to the wreck, which included how he'd personally look after showing him around.

Politeness, coupled with selective personal touch, worked too, Tanner had been told by the Baroness, and he smiled. He'd never seen her touch a non-Royal, but then again, that might be because others had never risen high enough to gain her public praise.

Maybe. Maybe not. Dunno, he thought.

Back on the *Sword*, he Ansibled his aide. She would be on her way shortly and would arrive on Ghayth in less than an hour, so he'd wait and she could accompany him on the trip to the wreck in the far southern hemisphere.

Until then, he sat and used Gallipedia to learn more about teleportation and why it hadn't yet been discovered and developed here in the galaxy.

Yet was the active word, he thought, and he read on.

The Caliph lolled on his comfortable chair, and with both feet up on the hassock in front of him, he almost rolled right off his chair. He grinned at that and slowly sat up to be only partially lying down, and his boots squeaked on the leather footstool.

"AI," he said to the room's artificial intelligence module, "is the vid all queued up and ready to play?"

"Yes, Your Excellency," it replied.

It had taken more than four years to get his hands on that tape, and finally it would be used today. Costs had been astronomical, and if it hadn't been for a Tillion administrative assistant who liked to play craps more than keeping secrets, it would have never come his way.

He smiled. He had the goods, and now to present them.

He hadn't bothered to tell his servants that the guest he was waiting for deserved any kind of refreshments, but now he thought better of that.

"AI, find me a steward," he said.

Across the room was an alcove that hid the doorway. Within a minute, the steward appeared. He quickly presented himself in front of the Caliph and said as sweetly as he was able to, "Yes, Your Excellency?"

The Caliph sat up a bit straighter and smiled at the young man, who at well more than six and a half feet in height was rail thin like most of the Caliphate citizens. He wore a modest plain brown uniform with the traditional arjak and its small icons of the Caliphate in indigo blue, and his blue boots shone like glass. As a non-Royal, his arjak could not be more than ten percent blue, but the young man looked like he was capable and a true Caliphate citizen.

"Your name," the Caliph asked.

"Your Excellency, my name is Adnan Abdul-Rahim, of the tribe of Rahim from the southern continent," he said proudly.

The Caliph nodded. The Rahim tribe was large, well respected, and owned many of the best casinos out on the RIM. "My guest today, Adnan, will be an Entiran from Tillion—about the same as an earl in our worlds. You will need to inquire as to what kind of refreshments a Tillion humanoid might like and serve them soon after he arrives. I leave it up to you to decide as to what and how many—you're the steward, Adnan. Ensure, however, that all protocols are followed and observed. You know what is said about Tillions ..." he instructed and then slouched back down as the steward bowed and left to hustle up some food and drink.

Tillions were different. Their single-planet realm lay only four lights off the southern border of the Caliphate. Caliphs going back at least four centuries, he knew, had courted them to join the Caliphate but had been rebuffed time and time again. Perhaps it was that as a humanoid race, the Tillions couldn't see how becoming a planet in the Caliphate would be of much value to them? Perhaps it was because the Caliphate citizen was usually six plus feet tall and the Tillions were only five feet plus a couple of inches. He snorted at that one; looking down on a person was something he'd always done unless there was an Eran in the room, as they were always twice as tall.

"Not height. It must have to do with the gender issue," he said to himself.

The Entiran visiting today was a male. No one— as far as he knew—had ever seen or met a female Tillion. He had visited the capital, Mancerat, only twice, but like all off-worlders, he had been barred from leaving the landing port. The city had only a few towers that stood above the landing port walls, and even studying the city itself when you came down was not instructional at all. There was no pedestrian traffic; all cars and flyers were totally closed, and like all off-worlders, he'd learned nothing about the planet.

Tillion was the only realm that lay between the Caliphate and the Duchy d'Avigdor, which were about ten lights apart; Tillion sat in the near center of that expanse. The duke, he'd learned years ago, had an open invitation to join the duchy sent to Tillion, but again it had been refused. They stood alone. "Until today, perhaps," he said to himself, as a Caliphate guard, a Ramat officer with polished boots, strode in and half turned to present the Tillion Entiran.

"Your Excellency, may I present the Entiran of Teuku, your visitor today," he said.

Must remind the Ramat that there is a protocol for introducing aliens. He smiled as he rose and went over to the short Tillion noble. Teuku was the major country on Tillion and a large nationalistic force.

He's maybe about five feet one inch tall. I wonder if he minds looking up to me? The Caliph thought. Tillion males were very fashionable, and the Entiran was no exception. The broad wide-brimmed hat on the alien's head was wider than the alien was. Polished metal scales of red and white made up a large part of his jacket, and his legs were encased in tight leather legs that tucked down into plain black boots. The Tillion's face was normal looking—if three eyebrows were normal, he thought. The alien appeared to be smiling at him. No teeth showed, but the corners of its wide mouth arched up, and the alien dipped his head to the Caliph as the head of state.

Sort of like a duke meeting a king, he thought and smiled. A duke for how much longer is the question.

He made his own small talk, led the Tillion over to the side seating area, and got him ensconced onto a divan that was very luxurious yet still had some support.

"Entiran, I greet you on behalf of the Caliphate and welcome you to my home, here on Neria," he said, and he studied the alien closely.

There was no movement to remove his hat, and he sat with his head tilted back a bit so that he could see the Caliph. Must be a part of the Tillion protocols, he thought. Should make for an interesting conversation.

The Tillion nodded, and small talk continued for a bit while each talked about how nice it was to meet once again. Three years ago, they had been a part of a larger task force that had been called together to help fight the alien reaper ships that had appeared over Memories and had been successfully sent packing.

The Tillion ship, the TN Fendi, had been a part of the overall Tillion Navy, but in fact, the Caliph now learned, it belonged to the Teuku state. It had, he remembered, played a vital role in destroying one of the alien reaper ships. Good to know, he thought, that the planet, while presenting a unified front to the RIM Confederacy, was still broken up at home into countries or states.

He smiled at that bit of news and filed it away under pride, realizing that like humans, the Tillions too had some similar characteristics. And he knew how to work on pride ...

"Entiran, yes, it is good that we meet again.I need to ask that the rest of our conversation be kept private—between you and me only. Could we agree to that simple start for today?" he asked.

The Tillion nodded, the large brim of his hat flopping a bit as he noted that confidentiality was to follow.

"Then let's get to it, shall we? You know that the Duchy d'Avigdor has recently lost its duke and that the Temporary Provisional Government has a short list of 'candidates' that they are considering to merge with to continue their existence, correct?"

The Tillion nodded and his hat brim did too.

"Then what you might not know is that while there are a few others on the list, the ones that count are the Caliphate and the Barony. And what I need from you is to help ensure that the Caliphate wins the Duchy d'Avigdor," he said quietly.

The hat brim tilted to one side as the Tillion took that in. "Caliph, you do know that I am not the head of state of Tillion. That is the Narrisol, and while there is no love lost between us, I doubt that Teuku can be of much assistance. Surely the head of state is the one you should be talking to, Caliph?"

The Caliph smiled and went on. "And what you say, while true, is exactly why I'm coming to you, Entiran. What I propose is not only to take over the duchy with your help but also to unseat the current Narrisol and make you the new head of state," he said, putting a bit of excitement into his voice. He'd done more persuading than most, and he knew how to use his voice to gain an advantage, and now was certainly just such a time.

"Entiran, a few things to consider? That Tillion lies between the Caliphate and the Duchy d'Avigdor. If we take over same, there might be a call to also take over Tillion. You would stand against that, of course. You would also know that you're POV would win the day no matter what things looked like to the rest of the RIM," he said as he held out one finger on a hand.

"Next," he said as the second finger was stuck out, "you would need to launch a Tillion-wide push on your planet to unseat the Narrisol and take his place because of his stance on the female problem, Entiran."

The wide-brimmed hat snapped backward as the alien jolted upright on the divan. "We do not have —we cannot even talk about—any 'female' problem. There is none," he said.

He looked like he was going to get up and quit the meeting. But he didn't, the Caliph thought, because of my offer to make him the new Narrisol.

The Caliph nodded and then held out a third finger. "The female problem is that Tillion has no females. Your race is uni-gendered and while that is unknown by anyone outside of Tillion, I know it," he said as he waved a hand.

The room AI turned on a vid screen on the wall beside them, and the black screen suddenly came alive. There was a tour of a medical facility—a birthing facility was what some of the Caliph's Ramat staff had called it. Thousands of tanks holding embryos at all stages of maturity stretched out as far as one could see. While the vid was only a minute or so in length, it captured the workers at the facility quite clearly. They were Tillions, even wearing their hats in the labs, but it was Tillion nonetheless.

The Entiran almost choked. "You know that this is ... this is espionage, Caliph," he said.

"Aye, I do. But should this make its way out into

the RIM, the Tillion membership might come into question as well as force at least a change in the head of state," he said carefully, now making his pitch. "What I will do, is to make this public at exactly the right time to the RIM.

"What you need to do is to begin a grassroots campaign on Tillion, to open up about this to the RIM. You need to position yourself against the Narrisol—and let the sudden publication of this vid speak for you. We know the Narrisol we know controls those facilities and makes his own state billions of credits based on the fact that Tillion is uni-gendered. You stand against that, and at the right time, you will become the new Narrisol as he falls."

"And how will that win you the Duchy d'Avigdor," the Entiran asked.

Got him, the Caliph thought. He wants the crown.

"We will make the vid appear to be a release of the duchy. That will cause them much anguish as well as loss of their superior reputation on the RIM, and then when they're at their lowest, we will offer to stand in their place and add the might of the Caliphate to their own support with the proviso that they join us. The bane of the RIM opposed to the strength of the Caliphate—their choice is an easy one to foretell. We will get the duchy, you the

Narrisol crown ..." he said as his voice trailed off, and he nodded to the alcove.

A group of stewards and their helpers entered the room with refreshments. The conversation stopped and the Caliph and the Entiran rose to look over the various items. The Caliph noted there were items he liked—the dates wrapped in that smoked beef and the hummus to dip into too. He took a small plate and then sat on the opposite divan as the Entiran chose carefully from other dishes and rejoined him.

They ate quietly and both accepted an iced tea too, and the room emptied back out.

"Good to see that your choices for us included only male-gendered species," the Tillion said.

The Caliph nodded and guessed he'd been correct when he'd glanced at the platters and noted the bright yellow male sardines and the Garnuthian ram stew as well. It was known that a Tillion—all Tillions—ate only male-gendered animal meats and fish; it was good to see that the steward had chosen well.

He finished his plate with a large spear of some kind of cheese and washed it down with a gulp of iced tea. As he straightened up, he spoke again. "Entiran. Do we understand each other?"

The Tillion nodded in agreement. "I will start a grassroots planet-wide movement to 'come clean' to the RIM on our gender issue. Incidentally, we did have women up until about three hundred years ago—a vicious virus came and took them all in less than a year. So we adapted and closed off our society, and using technology, we now breed all our young in tanks until their birth. I have four sons myself—our female young never are born successfully," he said, his voice almost catching, but he shook it off.

The Entiran took a deep breath and continued. "You will, yes, get some more vid from me with more about the breeding facilities for you to release. When you do that, the blame will fall on the Duchy d'Avigdor—and it will be seen as them against Tillion. The Narrisol will defend our position—and yes, I do think that war will be the solution that he will pick. And at the right time, I take it, you will offer to the duchy to help them out of their predicament. The Narrisol will be deposed—and I will rise to become the next Narrisol. Do I have that all correct, Caliph?"

He nodded.

He had it correct.

And almost right too, but that comeuppance would come later. Now the video needed to go to his IT team for final doctoring to make it look ten years old instead of a few months old.

Honeymoon Bottle

#####

She sat quietly at the window, having dragged a
chair over to it, and looked at the view before her.
She wondered if all the previous Master Adepts
had looked out this window at the much-changed
landscape before her: the abandoned farm with its
empty and broken-down buildings and barn; the
fields now overgrown with weeds, moss, and
fungus; and the corral with its wooden fences that
had missing pieces and looked like a crooked smile
from here.

Gloria raised her eyes to stare at the far horizon
and saw more farms too, all with the same lack of
farmers and crops. Climate change to Eons had
done this, and only now, almost a full six hundred
years after the change in their sun, were there signs
that the radiation levels were beginning to drop.

Those reports, of course, had been kept under
wraps so there would be no sudden interest by
speculators in buying up the thousands of deserted
farms that soon could be farmed again. She knew
this was the right thing to do—her economic
advisers had been drumming that into her weekly
reports now for months. But she also knew that the
planet's population would soon learn that truth as
the climate changed around them. Last winter had
been less severe than the previous couple of dozen
winters with less snowfall in the northern climes

and less spring flooding. That had meant that the overgrowth of weeds and secondary plants had been able to successfully seed for new growth. And she'd heard, via those weekly updates, that there was some talk from the university of some professors claiming this could only be a result of a change in the sunlight itself.

Those leading-edge professors had been brought here to the walled city about fifteen miles north of Dessau, the capital city of Eons, and she and some of her advisers has spoken to them. They had questioned the professors about why they'd argue in favor of their recent new views that something was up with the sunlight—and they'd been severely reprimanded by her. She had even been forced to threaten exile from Eons and the whole of the RIM Confederacy post-secondary education industry should they refuse to hide what it was they had guessed. Gloria had offered that they were right. The radiation was lessening—and by almost a full fourteen percent in the past year—but they had to plan for the changes that such a resurrection of their climate would cause before it was common knowledge.

She watched a hawk well above her rooms at the top of the walled city tower as he swung with the winds and soared with no wing strokes at all. Looking for his lunch, she thought, as he spun to the left and went on toward the fields ahead.

For a moment, she wondered what that kind of existence might be like, and then she shrugged and reached for the glass of water she'd balanced carefully on the window ledge. Taking a sip, she stood, went back to the facing loveseats in the room to sit, and put the glass on the table.

And she looked over at the wall facing her and noted the time; a clock was an old-fashioned way of telling time, she well knew, but one that worked easily. She wore no jewelry at all, like all Master Adepts, except for the necklace that held the icon of the Issian faith, a golden sphere representing a planet with rings around it. She fingered it and knew it was time. She closed her eyes as she began the traditional Issian mind linking.

She fell. She was not falling, she knew, but in her mind, she was falling, and falling into a blackness that was absolute. After a minute or so, a single point of light appeared ahead of her. It grew in size as she fell toward it, and after only a few more seconds, she joined the already linked minds of her inner circle.

She was seated—at least in this point of view— and in a circle around her were ten more Issians, one more than the normal complement. She nodded to them all, and a very small smile appeared on her face as she glanced at Bram Sander—the newest addition to the circle. She had made the choice with a bit of reservation, as adding him to the inner circle had been a suggestion, a request—almost a firm demand—from her predecessor. The previous Master Adept had been killed only some months back at the Royal wedding of Lord Scott and the Lady St. August. The previous Master Adept had known it was coming and allowed it to happen, which carried Gloria into complying with the request to add Bram to the circle. The old Master Adept had simply made the point that as Lord Scott was so much a foundation for all the changes coming to the RIM Confederacy, it made great sense to add his best friend Bram to the inner circle.

And that was true, she thought. Lord Scott had been the fulcrum for most of the recent changes and discoveries here on the RIM for almost a decade now—Bram would help their faith keep up with same, and perhaps, she half-smiled again, even ahead of the leading edge.

"We welcome you, Master Adept," all of the minds said in unison.

She nodded back to them even though they couldn't see that motion. "I thank you for your time today and today there is the one item only to discuss—well, there is a small matter too as well," Gloria said as she decided to tell her advisers about the climate changes on Eons.

The discussion went well, she thought, as each of them had agreed that the news about the change in the Eon's star's radiation output should remain for now, at least, as a secret to the general population. Then they moved onto the item that worried her still.

"You all know that at our linking of two weeks ago, I had asked for you all to look into helping me find the three other worlds where they had made some kind of advance attempts at settling same. Of course, that's my 'take' on their reasoning, but the information is pretty authoritative that they landed on Ghayth and three other worlds. So, if anyone has any new information on those three worlds, we'd all like to know ..." she said.

And she looked around the linked group.

Zara Patel leaned in a bit and spoke to them all. "Master, what you've asked for is such a hard thing to do—my sister Elia and I have been on four worlds since our last linking, and on each we've been searching minds for any 'hint' of something that might be about the Praix. Nothing is what we've found—and I can say with all honesty, that the heads of state we've talked to all know nothing about the ancients, Master. Not a single thing. Even conversation however gently nudged toward the existence of any kind of 'old cultures,' led us nowhere ..." she finished off and Elia, seated beside her, nodded.

Gloria took that in. Searching a head of state was certainly a good way to see what they knew—only such a supreme ruler might have such knowledge, and while Zara and Elia had focused on that as a good source, the fact that four more RIM Confederacy worlds, Thrones, Conclusion, DenKoss, and Juno were crossed off the list was not good news.

Others chimed in too.

Pavla Jelinek and her sister Jana reported the same lack of any kind of information about the ancients from Farth, Garnuth, and Takan. Others offered up more names, and the new number of planets crossed off the list hit twenty-two pretty quickly.

Gloria turned to Bram and raised an eyebrow.

He nodded back. "Master, yes, I too tried to find out any kind of recon on these other Praix worlds— and I too found not a single conscious thought, or even a hidden thought, from the two worlds I was on—Merilda and Carnarvon, Master. I think that we're all going to be 'striking out' when it comes to this quest, Ma'am," he said, and his point was well made.

The Master nodded and realized that with more than ninety worlds to query, it would take a bit more time, but even if every single world was crossed off the list of possible Praix outposts, the fact was there were three. Three in the RIM Confederacy, and she had to find them.

"Might I, Ma'am, make one more point," Bram thought quietly.

She nodded.

Bram continued. "It might be that on the wrecked ship on Ghayth, there would be some kind of a log or record of the other planets. My own experience," he said, as he looked at the rest of the inner circle, "is as a Navy officer—and a large part of that world is the storage of exactly this kind of planetary data in the ship's database. Might I have leave to see if such records exist on the Ghayth wreck, Master?"

She was perturbed that she'd not thought of that herself—and yet once again happy that she had risked much in adding Bram to the inner circle, and she smiled widely.

"Good idea, Bram. Please, yes, do search—but again with a degree of confidentiality so as to really hide what it is we're looking for—understand?" she thought with precision.

Bram nodded and added, "Yes, Ma'am."

She nodded back and thought to herself that if Bram could find the names of those planets on the wreck on Ghayth, that would help her immensely, and she would find a way to repay his initiative somehow.

Coming back from the wreck, Tanner stared, lost in thought, out the window of the *Sword*. Ayla, his aide, sat beside him, and while he was unaware of it, she had gauged his mood and sat quietly without interrupting his train of thought. The *Sword* flew just about at a thousand feet above the sea that separated the southern continent that was the home for the alien wreck and the northern continent where Base-1 lay. It was a trip of only three thousand miles, but he'd asked his pilot to take it slow, and there was still about an hour left of the return to the city. His EliteGuard team of six sat behind him, taking up a couple of rows on the *Sword*. They had been very aware that as there was full security on Ghayth, they didn't need to be so close to him all the time; they had left a buffer zone around him when they had visited the wreck.

He had been somewhat surprised by the wreck itself—not having been there in months—and he'd been unaware of how a real xeno team worked—very unaware, he had realized. All over the wreck were placards and easels holding up hand-lettered signage with information on whatever was needed. On the major path that ran the north-south access corridor of the ship for instance, every fifty feet or

so, a sign read, "This is Alpha Path #1," and all
paths branching off were labeled similarly but with
a number that was matched by the icons on the path
themselves. Doorways that hung above had signs
hung with simple descriptions of what lay within:
"Room holds sleeping perches" was one that had
made him smile with its "No idea what goes on in
here" note. He had walked and enjoyed Professor
Beedles and his way of offering up information. For
everything they went by, Professor Beedles began
every explanation with a caution that it was their
"current thinking" as to what was what. It could
change, he'd said many times, and more than a
dozen times, he had explained what something was
—and what they'd originally thought about it too.

   He'd nodded.

   He knew that a Royal seldom asked real drill-
down questions, but he'd learned that the same
information could be gotten from his aide. Letting
her know when he wanted that kind of depth on an
area was a chore at first, but he'd quickly clued in
Ayla. Now when he said, "Now that's interesting,"
she would make a note and ask for more
information afterward. He'd get the information
directly from her later.

   This being a Royal was a job in and of its own
self. Learning how is not so much fun, he thought
for the twelfth time today, as he watched the swells

in the ocean far below.

He turned to Ayla and smiled at her.
"Lieutenant, can I ask that you add one more thing to the list of items I'd like to know more about?" he said.

"Aye, My Lord," she answered and got out a tablet and waited ready to type it in.

"I would like to know if there has been, as yet, any testing on power fluctuations around or near the bridge door when the alien's transporter suddenly works? Any kind of electrical or power irregularity at all? Surely, it takes power to do that, and I wonder if the xeno team might have thought of that as yet?"

She nodded as her fingers flew on the tablet, and moments later she said, "Yes, My Lord, I will have that information for you before dinner this evening too."

He nodded, turned back to his left in the window seat of the passenger area behind the bridge of the *Sword*, and smiled down at the ocean below. Its crests and swells were almost the same gray as the sky above. At this moment, it wasn't raining, but if he knew anything about Ghayth, he knew the rains came often. He wondered on that for a moment and then shook his head. There was no way anybody — even the superior aliens whose ship they were investigating — could control a whole planet's weather and make Ghayth so dreary and rainy. No way. That thought stuck with him, and he made a mental note to ask someone who might know about same.

Ayla cleared her throat beside him. "My Lord, we're approaching Base-1, and might I offer that I've made arrangements for you to have the penthouse suite at the big new hotel in town—the Ghayth-Hilton I'm told it's called. Your security detail will follow and be on the floors below too, and I've also asked that they empty the two floors below you of everyone else. Our transport is a simple troop carrier, and I am sorry about that, My Lord—"

He interrupted her as he laid a hand on her arm. "Ayla, not a problem. You've done well, and I can ride on an Oved if needs be," he said.

"That would be something to see," Ayla said, stifling a giggle.

He imagined she'd pictured him way up high on the back of the ten-foot tall elk-like animal with huge horns and feet the size of snowshoes. He almost grinned himself, and then he sighed as the *Sword* touched down on the landing pad and coasted to a stop.

He smiled as his EliteGuard team surrounded him and escorted him off the ship, down the landing ramp, and across the tarmac to the troop carrier. Two of the guardsmen offered him a hand up, and he shook his head as he jumped up onto the pipe ladder and hoisted himself up and into the rear of the bus. Moments later, they were trucking across the tarmac, weaving around a couple of ships —one of which was a Faraway frigate. Odd, he thought, but then he noticed there were Provost guards manning the gate access to the base, and he smiled at that. Good to see that security was important and a part of the SOP of the base. Must commend Commander Williams on that later at dinner.

The short trip to the new hotel took only a few minutes more, and twenty minutes later, he was soaking in his tub, the water jets swirling hot bubbles around him. He was upset he'd not thought to ask for a cold beer or a cold drink of some kind as he soaked and washed away the sweat from his trip to the wreck.

An hour later, he presented himself—along with his EliteGuardsmen—to the maître d' of the beautiful restaurant downstairs in the hotel. He was led over to a large corner table, and he grinned at his dinner guests.

"Major Stal, how nice," he said as he reached out a hand, and the marine in front of him took his hand and shook it vigorously. A friend now for years, the Major Alver Stal was the head of the

151

marine forces on Ghayth and had also been in the wedding party. They had shared much from beers to tumult.

The major spoke briefly in Tanner's ear as he pulled himself up close to his friend. "My sympathies on recent events, My Lord, but so, so good to see you up and around, Lord Scott."

Tanner nodded and then said his hellos to Commander Williams and Professor Reynolds, and everyone sat down and got settled.

The EliteGuards spread out on the two open sides of their corner area but not close, and Tanner noted that almost a full half of the tables in the restaurant were empty as a buffer around them. Ayla, he noted, sat over at the bar, and she had told him that all he'd need to do would be to catch her eye, and she'd come over instantly to help with whatever was needed.

The others were already having cocktails, so he smiled at the server who was hovering close by and ordered a glass of white wine. He knew that it would taste wonderful, but no alcohol would ever reach his bloodstream as he'd had the alcoholic vaccine that made him invulnerable to its allure.

They talked. And they talked about the Barony Navy, the RIM Navy, the Faraway and Leudie trade wars recently fought, and of the latest rugby standings of various RIM Confederacy teams.

152

Nobody was surprised that Tanner was a fan of the Andros Avengers, the home team of the Halberd planetary capital. s

Alver grinned and prodded him with their late lack of many wins. "And if you think the Avengers are going to be any better later in the season, you've just got to go and see a game and note that they traded away the best Loose Head Prop in the RIM Confederacy league for an Openside Flanker who broke his leg in his first game. Now they lose every scrum, and even the few they do win, there's no one to pick up what the Hooker hooks back to the next row," he said, and he smiled at them all.

All knew that as a citizen of Gazaya, one of the Barony realm planets, Alver was very partial to his own team, the Grazers. Often, he'd beg off socializing if there was a game on with his team, and instead, he would find a spot to sit and watch the rugby game, cheering for his team.

Tanner smiled, nodded, and offered up that the Avengers, yes, had made some mistakes; however, the new general manager had made a promise to rebuild in the next year's draft. Tanner continued, "As the team is doing so bloody bad, they should be in the top couple of teams making choices in the first draft rounds."

More conversation and drinks followed, and as Tanner had expected, the cocktails were definitely a social lubricant and loosened everyone, except for him, up somewhat.

He made sure to offer up his kudos to one and all, as a good Royal should do. He complimented Commander Williams with his honest evaluation of the general sense of opportunity here on Ghayth, the success of the pioneer program, and the accompanying huge swell in buildings and new trade too.

He thanked the professor for the xeno team itself and mentioned how he knew they would make great strides in understanding the alien technology —and bring it within the grasp of the Barony to take charge of same.

He also smiled at Alver and added that he knew the major would look after security planet-wide, which was exceptionally important to one and all— especially to the Baroness.

He laughed when they did, and he smiled and nodded a lot. While the white wines had tasted delightful, he did not get a single bit of buzz. Must thank Doctor Etter for that, he thought and shied away from the intruding thought about his sister Gia and her recent move to the Barony Hospital Ship.

More than enough time for that later. He grinned at his dinner companions and listened to another of Alver's rugby stories. Tanner enjoyed the camaraderie and laughter, which allowed him to temporarily put any thoughts of the Duchy d'Avigdor and its offer From his mind.

#####

The package came off the RIM Navy courier ship, as one of thousands to be delivered to the Duchy d'Avigdor every single day. It was tagged, as they all were, with a chip that offered every single item one might want to know about the sender and the route the package had followed to get to Neen City from wherever it had come from. And every single piece of information coded on that chip was untrue. False. Not a speck of veracity was on that chip—which was exactly what the sender had planned for to begin with.

It was a small package. Not more than a foot long and a couple of inches wide, it was wrapped with a very eye-catching pattern of violet and neon yellow stripes. It weighed less than a pound, and it was un-crushable too. Nobody could squeeze the package to feel what might have been inside.

The package had been on the courier ship for more than a week. Courier ships were the last ones to receive the new Barony Drive installs, and this one, the RN Trump, had yet to be outfitted with same. So it had been in transit for twelve days since it had left Conclusion with stops at Neria in the

Caliphate, Tillion, then Anulet, and finally Neen.
Each stop had been rather short with only enough
time to dump out the containers with incoming
packages and items and then pick up the outgoing
containers for on-ship sorting and then storage until
the proper planets were landed upon.

On the tarmac, robo-bots placed the containers on
top of matching railcars, which were linked up to be
driven off by a human. The driver did grunt at least
twice, as some of the containers seemed to be
improperly filled, and even in front of the long line
of carts, he could hear things falling inside the
newly attached containers.

"Not my worry," the driver said to himself as he
kicked the pedal down, and the whole container
train jumped ahead. He wheeled it around a Leudie
trader ship, two Lurdar freighters that were getting
new anti-grav plates, and an Alex'n sphere ship
that was just about ready to take off.

The driver headed the train toward the bright
green building across the tarmac on the landing
port, and in less than a minute more, the driver
wheeled the train into the side door and hit the
brakes almost immediately. He heard more shifting
cargo behind him, but didn't care as usual.

Once settled, he picked up his cargo tablet,
bounced off the driver's seat, and took the stairs
two at a time up to the receiving office. Inside the

door, he grinned at the man seated behind the counter and smiled. "Billy, Billy ... last load in from the Trump, all accounted for," he said.

"We'll let the reports speak for themselves, Matthew," he answered as he held out his hand for the tablet. A few minutes later, after running a report and downloading the data to his own console, he smiled and nodded. "You're right, Matthew ... all here and all scanned and ready for the sorters," he answered as the driver left the office, done for the day.

The train of containers had already been unhooked from the engine and now was disappearing off to the left as the railcars were wheeled ahead and inside the large interior of the green courier building. Once inside, the containers were to be opened, contents sorted for their addressees, and then scheduled for drone or manual delivery. Some packages were numbered as one package out of a series of packages, and they had to all be gathered together for a single stop. Some were marked FRAGILE and had to be inspected to ensure that at this point, at check-in on Neen, they were still in good order. Some had to be handled separately as they had a RUSH sticker, which meant they were to go out first. Most, of course, did not have such a sticker and were going to be general delivery only. A few—a very few—

were marked SECURITY FIRST, and they went to
the head of the line as they were pulled from the
flow of parcels and placed in the hands of a Duchy
d'Avigdor Provost guard who had drawn that duty
today.

So far, looking down, he saw only three such
packages—two in the normal bright red cardboard
envelopes marked for delivery to NEEN
CUSTOMS and one in violet and neon yellow
stripes marked AMBASSADOR BEDRE.

"Three," he said to himself, "that should be nice
and easy. A stopover at Customs, and then run
downtown to the government buildings to drop this
off for Bedre. Then off to the pub for a beer. Great
way to end the day." He grinned to himself as he
picked up the three items and went out the back
door.

He smiled at another of the guards who was
having a suntan session in the late summer month.
He put on his helmet, swung a leg over the saddle
of his bike, and slapped his thumb down on the
start plate. As the bike roared into life, he made
sure that the saddlebags were sealed on the three
parcels. He gunned the throttle, and the bike roared
down the rear alley. Soon, he was out on the street,
headed to Customs first.

Once he'd tossed the two envelopes into the
hands of the Customs clerk and gotten a

thumbprint on his tablet proving the two packages were delivered, he was back on his bike and on his way downtown. He roared along, enjoying the summer sunshine on the tall buildings ahead as he made his way down the parkway and the traffic got heavier.

"Watch out for the turkey-faces," he said to himself and thanked, for the millionth time, his uncle who had taught him how to ride a bike and watch out for other drivers all the time.

Ahead of him, a car in his lane was turning left, and he slowed. Noting the hole in the traffic in the lane on his right, he leaned right and the bike leaned too. The car that had been slowing to turn left suddenly jumped into the right turn lane without signaling.

"Turkey-face," he said to himself as he jammed on the rear brake to spin the rear end out to the right. He laid down the bike on its left side and realized the road would grind his leg badly, but at this point, it was only a leg. He jammed the front brake on full with a grip that almost bent the handlebars. He closed his eyes as his helmet struck the parkway pavement, and he passed out.

The bike, with its large cross-section now on the pavement, scraped and screamed as its metal frame slowed quickly but still struck the car with a severe blow, and it bounced off the bike, into the curb, and then hit the car one more time, which drove it into the guardrail with a huge crash.

It was a mess, and all the parkway traffic came to a complete stop.

Parts of the bike, including the broken saddlebags, lay strewn around the wreck of the car, its bumper detached, as it smoldered, and the driver jumped out quickly for safety. Someone ran up to the bike as it lay still running, and the rpms were revving up higher and higher. That Good Samaritan couldn't find a way to turn the bike off, but he dragged the rider off the seat and away from the crash site.

Someone yelled for a medical doctor, and from the other side of the parkway, a man hoisted himself up and over the median guardrail, identified himself as a doctor, and ran to the bike rider to help. Maneuvering around the broken parts, he kicked an exhaust pipe to the curb where it came to a rest against a badly smashed violet and neon yellow package.

No one noticed the package, even with the neon yellow and violet stripes. Everyone was focused on trying to help the rider, and in the distance, one could hear sirens from medical and law enforcement vehicles drawing closer.

CHAPTER SIX

The Baroness was pleased with the executive committee room, which she thought of as hers. She noted that, as usual, there were seven carefully spaced spots around the round table, each with its own desk pad, Agenda, writing items, and charging pads for a user's tablet. The room had been plain when she'd been appointed to the committee a few years back; however, she had been able to use her influence to convince the Navy Hall staff to liven the room up. Once they had learned she would donate some tchotchkes to help liven up the space a bit, they readily agreed.

A nice native Ikarian carving was on the brick wall opposite her seat at the table. Its feathered serpent of orange and red on the animal's yellow skin added a real whoop of color. The bookcases that lined the whole wall behind her now had more decorative items. Knickknacks from Ttseen and carvings of real sailing ships from DenKoss lined some of the shelves. Small powered trinkets from Carnarvon that occasionally flashed a soft red glow were placed around little carvings. A glass jar of small beads and sand stars from Merilda sat in front of some leather-bound books.

She tossed her hair as she waited. "While the room is fine now, perhaps it was the people on the committee who met each month here that bothered me the most," she said to herself, reflecting on each member individually.

The Caliph was the Caliph. He wore his ambitions on his sleeve, and she knew more than enough about how to handle him.

Chairman Gramsci was still an unknown. She had been trying to fathom him and his own desires now for almost ten years. She still was unable to figure out what drove the alien, and thus, she was not yet able to control him.

Admiral McQueen, the chief of staff for the committee was someone she knew and understood well. McQueen was a force with great experience and knowledge about how to navigate not only the stars but the kind of bureaucracy the RIM Confederacy was all about.

The new Master Adept was still something of an

unknown. She knew the woman could read her mind, but she also knew that it meant that there was often synergy between what the Barony wanted and the Issians wanted.

The Doge of Conclusion was a real non-player, and as usual, he went with the flow around the table.

And the last seat, still vacant now for almost six months, was the one that used to hold the Duke d'Avigdor, who had died at her stepdaughter's wedding. The Duchy d'Avigdor was the prize, and she expected to win it.

She nodded and smiled up at the admiral who walked in just as she finished analyzing the committee members

"Baroness," he said, "nice to see you here so early, Ma'am. And an overall thank you once again for the Barony Drive—we all can now be early for just about anything."

She had no idea, really, if that was a slur on her release of the new drive or not, but at face value, perhaps he meant it, and so she kept the smile on her face.

"Admiral—so nice to see you too. And yes, the new drive has helped out immensely with travel here on the RIM, but perhaps as we release it inwards, it will help much of this arm of the galaxy too," she said. She really had no intention of doing that kind of overall release, but nobody should know that, and her smile stayed on her face as though painted on.

"Undoubtedly, Ma'am. Good for the Barony," he said as he dropped his folders, tablet, and pile of other items onto the desk pad in front of him. His position was to her right with one other, the Master Adept, between them, and moments later as he was still trying to get his items organized, the Doge of Conclusion and the Master Adept appeared together and greeted them all.

It took still another ten minutes for the Caliph and the chairman to show up and get organized too. At last, she thought, everyone is here. Once he had taken his seat, the chairman called the meeting to order.

The committee clerk rose. "Agendas are at your places, and we only have one more addition—the new item will be in the new business category at the end, number seven, and I will pass out the proposal when we reach that spot," the clerk said, and she sat as the meeting began.

The Baroness couldn't care less about the current state of the trade wars between the Leudies and the Faraway realms, but she listened dutifully and nodded where applicable. This was old news and in fact, the release of the Barony Drive had kept these two realms within the RIM Confederacy. She mentally checked off that she had been the single saving grace for these two alien planets and the rest of the executive committee knew that.

Items two, three, and four were of little interest to her. Under item two, the realm of Hope was asking again for more RIM funds to help them cope with rising sea levels. Novertag, which was item three, was going through a large expansion of its naval yards and was looking for RIM Navy business. On the Agenda again, but at number four this time, was Duos asking for help with their civil war campaigns.

The easiest vote for everyone on the committee was the fourth item. Not helping either side was the mantra at the table, and she voted the same as the rest of them.

The Baroness quietly tapped her toe as she waited for the committee to move through Agenda items five and six. Randi was asking for some leeway on the customs for their magnetite exports as item number five, and everyone agreed more details and further study were required before a decision could be made. For the sixth Agenda item, Quaran was also looking for relief on its latest exports for its Beaujolais Nouveau for the upcoming season.

Finally, an item that is of some interest to me, she thought and grinned inwardly as she was all for great wine. The Baroness voted for same after speaking about what a great way it'd be to help the farmers of Quaran to make a better living. She owned, through several off-planet surrogate companies, controlling interest in a large wine exporter, but she didn't think that was important enough to mention. The Quaran request passed easily.

Throughout the first six Agenda items, the Baroness waited patiently until the committee moved on to the new business. The clerk rose and handed out the new items on its own sheet, and as the Baroness was given hers, she couldn't help but frown.

Duchy business. I knew it.

Chairman Gramsci spoke first, and while his tones were measured and rational, it was the import of what he was saying that counted for some in the room. "The Temporary Provisional Government of the Duchy d'Avigdor has asked that we make everyone aware of the current search for their new realm partner," he said.

She noted he didn't even look at the sheet of paper before him. He knew about it beforehand, she realized, and that too was an issue. She had three moles within the executive committee staff and not one had said a thing to her about this.

"We have kept this on the down-low as they say

—at least as humans say, I might add—so that no one would learn of this up front," he said.

She nodded at that. Still should have found out earlier though, she thought.

"Here's the gist of what they want us to know. They originally had a list of six realms that they had chosen to begin to have talks with. The names on that list are held in the strictest confidence—but I'm doing away with that as of right now. Both the Caliphate and the Barony are on that list. Genie, the last one to be added, has actually turned down the offer. Hope has done the same thing as well. The Duchy itself has crossed off Thrones and Merilda as potential merge realms. Technically, that leaves only the Caliphate and the Barony," he said, and he leaned back. One hand toyed with a gavel while he crossed two more on his stomach as he wiped his brow with another.

He pointed at the Baroness and then the Caliph. "We know—now at least—that the duchy will belong to one of you. Six planets gained by one of you—which may make for some interesting times here on the RIM," he finished up, all six hands now lying flat on the desk pad in front of him.

The Baroness looked over at the Caliph and then dipped her head, so he spoke first.

"I take it then, that the Option Number Two as was presented at the full Confederacy Council meeting last month—the codicil whereby a new heir might be named—is also gone by?"

Figures, she thought, that he'd go to that first.

The chairman shook his head. "We have no idea on that. It may still be in play, we only know what Ambassador Bedre passed on to us. I have no real inkling either on that., The heir may still be under consideration like the other two or not. No idea," he said.

She could tell he at least looked like that was what he meant. She thought on that too for a minute before she nodded to the chairman and finally spoke.

"I thank you too," she said nicely and politely, even though the Caliph had not done so, "on the news, Chairman. We, yes, are one of the realms on that list, and now that it's shrunk to only the two of us, we will both need to watch carefully for any kind of conflict of interest," she said. Or what might appear to be same even though behind the scenes, I am working to win the duchy.

The chairman nodded and then said, "I will notify the Duchy d'Avigdor's Temporary Provisional Government, via Ambassador Bedre, that we have now gotten the current status of the duchy's position and the Committee is aware. We will also make this an Agenda item for the next full RIM Confederacy Council too with your permission ..."

He received a clear-cut sign of agreement all around the table, and the meeting was adjourned.

Taking the elevator down to the ground floor of Navy Hall, the Baroness caught the eye of the new Master Adept and smiled. She got a big return smile and wondered what the Issian had seen behind all that posing and posturing at the committee meeting.

The Lady St. August sat down lightly at the table and looked around at the group she had assembled.

And not a single had been used either, she thought and smiled inwardly at that. Trying to keep this meeting quiet and confidential had been a bit difficult, and the only reason she'd been able to do so was because she had yelled — actually yelled — at her EliteGuard colonel.

He'd not wanted to do away with what he called SOP — standard operating procedure — whereby anybody entering the palace needed to be vetted first, then pass through security, and then be in sight of a guardsman at all times.

She had yelled at him and reminded him that the Barony did have an outpost over on ITO; he could very much end up there in charge of four corporals and give up his position and rank.

He'd complied instantly, and she had to remember that a personal attack worked best sometimes; not often, it was true, but it did work.

The EliteGuard colonel had met the *Sword*, the personal ship of Lord Scott, as it had pulled into the navy landing base here on Neres just hours ago and had hustled the few occupants away from the ship into a troop carrier and the privacy within. Half an hour later, the carrier had pulled up at the palace and backed in at one of the many service entrances. The colonel escorted the four occupants through several corridors, up staircases, and even up an escalator too. Eventually, they reached this meeting room, which was little more than a small salon; as of today, the room held this large round table and six chairs.

Each took a seat and waited. They knew what to expect, and all were quietly waiting.

One chair held Professor Klaasjan Boven of the university on Carnarvon, the acknowledged expert on RIM Confederacy law and the constitution that bound all the realms together. He knew what the meeting was about and had brought in a large binder of documents, which he placed in front of him at the table.

One chair held Ambassador Bedre of the Duchy Temporary Provisional Government, representing the Duchy d'Avigdor. He was fidgeting with his tablet, and the Lady thought that was normal since he had no idea why he had been invited.

One chair held the new Barony fleet admiral, Admiral Higgins, who wore his five stars with pride, and he was at the table to represent the Barony and her military forces. He'd only been with the Barony now for a few days, but he was well known to have been able to parse what was necessary for any man's navy in less time.

The Lady herself sat next as the table was laid out, and beside her was an empty chair.

The last chair at the table held Prime Minister Kondo Lazaro of Amasis. He too was unaware of why he'd been asked to attend the meeting, but he was savvy enough to smile at anyone who caught his eye. Kondo was a good friend to her husband, and the Lady thought he was going to be helpful, should she need to look for help persuading her husband of his good friends.

The door opened and in walked Lord Scott who did a double take as he took in the people already within the room. He smiled at them all as he took the only empty seat.

"Well, nice to see you all again—and Professor … Professor Boven, yes?" he said as he looked across the table at the only one present that he didn't really know.

The professor bowed his head and said, "Yes, My

Lord, it is I—and I am pleased to have been invited to this meeting."

Helena noted that her husband just nodded and then turned to her.

"And this meeting is for ..." he said nicely, as he had no idea.

But he is soon to learn, she thought. "Lord Scott," she said quite formally, "yes, I called this meeting to discuss your acceptance of the late Duke d'Avigdor's will as you become the new duke according to his codicil."

Nobody in the room said a word.

She waited a full minute before continuing. "To all here, you should know the following. That the late duke died, but in his will," she said as she pointed at the thick folder in front of her, "he added a codicil just a few months back. That if Lord Scott wishes to accept the late duke as his adopted father, then the dukedom will fall to Lord Scott as his heir. Simple. Neat. And yet, as I'm sure some of you here have just realized, very much a strange set of circumstances. We are here today to discuss just that. That if Lord Scott agrees to the codicil and accepts that he be adopted by the late duke, then he will become the heir—and all that this position entails," she said quietly.

"Questions ... I'm sure that many of you have questions, but before you ask, may we hear from

Professor Boven first," she said.

Each of the meeting participants nodded.

Professor Boven half-smiled and opened his binder. Using a tab, he drilled down about halfway in the binder. "Most of what we assume will be the biggest hindrance of such an acceptance is the simple fact that the duke is no longer alive. He is dead. So how can he 'adopt' anyone would be what we think is the major sticking point. And we have an answer for that too," he said, and he pulled the binder closer so he could refer to same.

"Over the past thousand years that the RIM Confederacy has been in existence, there have been two times previously when such a set of events—not exactly the same but similar—have occurred," he said as he looked at the circled faces around him.

"First, back six hundred years ago, in the Barony itself, a baron passed away, and his illegitimate son was not as yet born, but he inherited anyways. Yes, there were court battles, and, yes, there was more conversation than one might imagine, but the son was born and inherited the Barony. That would, we feel, press home the point that someone can inherit a Royal title, regardless if the one offering up the title is alive or not."

He shuffled down a couple of pages then and stopped once more. "Point two is the case of the Caliph who inherited the title about one hundred and fifty years ago, and it reinforces the same item. Seems that the Caliph in power, with over a hundred wives and perhaps five hundred children, did not want any of his children to inherit the title. So he had his will include a codicil, whereby any Caliphate citizen who could scale their huge Mount Makalu, in less than one day, would be named his son—and inherit. I know, I know, gender specific and the rest of the arguments, but in fact, more than a hundred young men died trying that. But one did make it—the records show that he had nine minutes to spare, but he climbed that solid ten-thousand-foot-high ice mountain in less than a day. And he was named the new Caliph."

The attendees were restless, and he realized that, Helena saw, but she did not interrupt him.

"Yes, I know, but that instance shows us that someone can inherit a title having no regard for any kind of bloodline either. This, too, helps our case," he said, and he closed the binder.

"What we have are two precedents for inheriting a Royal title—both from a title holder who was dead. As far as I am concerned, in any kind of RIM Confederacy Supreme Court case, the precedents speak for themselves. The late duke can will—and did will—the title to Lord Scott. If he wants it, it's his, and I stake my reputation on the court case being settled in Lord Scott's favor." He pushed the binder away from him and looked at the faces around him.

Admiral Higgins cleared his throat. "In the case of the Barony title, the illegitimate son carried the bloodline of the Barony, and surely that fact would make it easier to see as a successful item," Admiral Higgins said, more as a question than a statement.

Professor Boven nodded and said, "Yet while that is true, it's the result of a dead Royal's codicil. The will has power that the dead Royal no longer has ... do you see that, Admiral?"

Admiral Higgins nodded in response, and the Professor looked around the table.

Ambassador Bedre nodded too. "I follow and concur, Professor. Your own research backs up our own—there is no way that bequeathing a Royal title in one's will makes it any less of a normal codicil. As we said months back directly to Lord Scott—if he wants the duchy, it is his," he said quietly.

Prime Minister Lazaro spoke up then. "So let me see if I understand this. A person—a Royal in this case—can leave his title to anyone he chooses. And if it is accepted by the recipient, then the title moves to that person. Right?" he asked, his voice slightly up in tone at the end.

Helena had no idea if Kondo was questioning the right of her husband to accept the title or if he was questioning something of a personal nature.

"Do you doubt the findings of the Professor, Kondo?" she said, using his first name to be more personal.

He shook his head. "No, My Lady, not at all ... it's just going to be a real stretch, I think, for most of the citizens of the Confederacy to accept such a thing, I might think," he said.

Tanner leaned forward. "That's even if I do want to do this, Kondo ... but the facts are as Professor Boven has presented them. I could take the dukedom and the duchy would be mine," he said, his voice trailing off at the end.

Helena knew he'd not yet decided, but she also knew she needed to add just a bit more fuel to her fire. "Admiral—can you see any problems, or troubles, in combining the Barony and the Duchy d'Avigdor from a navy point of view?"

His head tilted to one side, as he thought about just that for a minute or so, and then he nodded to her. "Ma'am, I see no problems. The Barony has currently almost thirty-three ships now online—the duchy I believe about twenty," he said as he looked over at Ambassador Bedre and received a nod in response.

"With over twenty-five thousand Barony Navy personnel plus more than ten thousand marines and air force members, we'd simply add in the duchy forces, and all would be fine. Well, there'd be some hiccups, yes, and some new SOP items to contend with, but on the whole, navy issues are non-existent if the Barony and the Duchy d'Avigdor become one, Ma'am," he said.

Having the admiral chime in was a good thing, Helena thought, and she smiled back at him.

"And Amasis, with its huge manufacturing industry, would you say that the addition of the Duchy d'Avigdor to our realm would cause any kind of economic issues, Kondo? In fact, as we see it, you would become the head of the combined economic faction for this new merge."

He shook his head. "No, Ma'am, not in the least. Dover and Waterloo, both duchy planets with big similar manufacturing capabilities like our own, would be a great merge with us. And more than that, we'd be greatly happy to have that extra technical ability as well at our beck and call, Ma'am," he said.

Helena checked off the constitutionality checkbox, the military one, and the economic one. All positive and all able to be worked out should there be any arising issues. She looked over at her husband who had sat quietly listening and taking it in.

He returned her gaze, and she was surprised to see a very slight shaking of his head. "I would like to thank you all for your efforts on this matter,"

Tanner said, and he made sure to catch each person's gaze as he went on.

"But at this point, I do not want to proceed any further. I have not made up my mind on this matter, and I believe I have, what, about eight more months to make up my mind, yes, Ambassador?"

The Ambassador nodded his positive response.

"Fine. Then I'd ask that you please keep this confidential. At this point in time, I'm thinking that I will not go ahead with this acceptance, but the next few months will allow me to make a final pragmatic decision. Thank you all, and especially thanks to the Lady St. August for working so hard to keep this away from me until today," he said, and he had that silly grin on his face, Helena saw.

She smiled at him, rose, and took him by the hand as they left the room together ... leaving the rest of the group to be shepherded by the EliteGuard colonel who had the task to sneak them all out without anyone seeing them.

Bottle was not the kind of planet one would imagine would have large, impressive government buildings and administrative infrastructure, but as the Baroness came down the ramp off the BN Compass, she learned she was only partially correct. Visiting the planet's actual capital, Corinth,

178

meant she was in unknown territory. She usually visited one of the resorts for a week or two on vacation each year. But today, the Compass had set down at the landing port in Corinth, and she was semi-impressed.

A head of her, the Compass captain led the way down the ramp to meet with the greeting group of Bottle government officials. As she walked in her heeled boots, she was careful of her steps, and she held out an arm for support to the EliteGuard at her immediate left. She'd requested him to be there, and she knew that she looked a bit overdressed, somewhat more girly than usual, and not very confident or authoritative as she walked with slow steps, watching the deck below her feet.

At the bottom of the ramp, she let go of the guardsman's arm and stepped forward to be presented by her captain to the waiting officials. A quick glance at them showed her that her opening gambit had worked—they all thought she was somewhat less than her reputation said. She had needed help in walking down a ship's landing ramp —that worked well, she thought as she smiled and nodded as the introductions were made.

The Bottle Premier, one Harley Cooper, still had his one eyebrow cocked as he leaned forward to bow to her.

She smiled at him. "Premier, so nice for you to

come out to meet with me in person," she said.

His face showed a painted-on smile as he nodded back to her. "Ma'am, we are honored that you'd visit Bottle, and we'd like to make you feel comfortable," he replied as he half-turned to escort her to the row of limos on the landing pad tarmac.

His chauffeur opened up a rear door on one, and she made her way into the comfortable back seat while he went around to the other side and got in.

She nodded a lot. Oh, she did hear him prattle on about how proud Bottle was that she—well, the Barony perhaps, he said as he corrected himself— had purchased that new resort, were running it, and how successful it was, and how much he'd heard good reports. Blah, blah, blah, she thought and yet continued to smile at him.

As the limo moved along the small tarmac area, through the gates to the field, and then down a broad landscaped street, she looked out the window and smiled. "Are we going to your offices, Premier?" she inquired.

He nodded. "Yes, Ma'am. We wanted to provide you with an official setting for whatever it is you might want to discuss," he said.

She shook her head. "Not needed, really, Premier. Instead, why don't we just pick out a local restaurant—with a nice outdoor patio—and have lunch together, just you and me?" she said. Her aides had come up with the names of five such restaurants, and she already had undercover EliteGuards at all five, carefully salted with the real customers.

He looked surprised but then leaned back, and in a few seconds, he replied. "Yes, Ma'am, that would be a nice surprise. Why don't I see if my aides can arrange just that kind of private lunch at, say, the Gremlin or the NorthSeas—both have great patios —right here in the city?"

She nodded as he quickly used the limo intercom to get that started.

The limo went on for a bit and then spun to the left to go down a wide boulevard that paralleled the waterfront. There were enormous hotels on their right and the sea on their left, and she was truly amazed at how beautiful Bottle was. It was a new experience, which she'd missed when she flew in to a resort well to the south.

As the limo pulled up to a restaurant that rose a couple of stories on their left, the premier spoke again as he hung up the intercom. "Ma'am, we've gotten a very private table at Gremlins—this is it. But it's up on the top—the second floor—and they have no escalator or elevator. Will that be okay?" he asked.

She smiled at him and nodded. Good to see that he was remembering that she'd needed support—

would keep him off balance. She followed him up the outer stairs to the patio.

After being seated and looking around, she was happy with their location. They sat at a private table tucked into a part of the patio that jutted out toward the beach below with no one closer than at least thirty feet. Seated at the closest two tables were her undercover guardsmen, and no one else sat any closer.

She smiled at the premier. "This is perfect, Premier. Might I suggest that we forgo any alcoholic beverages at this point and just have something cold? An iced tea perhaps or a fruit-ade of some kind? I'll leave it to you to choose, " she said and smiled at him again.

Showing the premier that she was a woman who relied on a man to make the decisions and that she needed physical support at times were important to her reason for her visit and part of her plan, little did he know.

He ordered two iced teas, and they sipped on them as he told her about the importance of their tourist-based economy and how it was, again, so nice that she had taken over her new resort.

She nodded. "Premier, I thank you for the kind words on our recent purchase. As you know, Lord Scott and Lady St. August spent more than two months there for their honeymoon recently—and the remoteness was an important piece of his recuperation from the events at their wedding. But more than that, Premier, is what I've been considering since we became the owner of that resort, which is my reason for my visit here today. I want Bottle to join the Barony—and I expect to get a positive answer from you here today," she said nicely.

His eyebrows arched up as far as they could go, and an expression of surprise was frozen on his face. This was no surprise to her, but before he could even say a word, she held up a hand to stop him.

She nodded to the table where two aides sat with two of her EliteGuards, and one of the aides rose to come over to stand beside her. She handed her a fat folder of documents and a tablet and then she retreated to her own table.

His eyebrows couldn't arch up any farther, the Baroness thought, as the Premier noted the documents and tablet in front of the Baroness.

The Baroness slid the folder toward him and then clicked a few buttons on the tablet as a vid began to play. What appeared to be a standard tourist video for Bottle played for a few seconds. A spreadsheet with a report on the planet replaced it. The Premier leaned in to look at it, and once again, she held up her hand to stop him from replying.

"This is a report about Bottle. Your economy, GNP, planetary debts, and forecasts. Most importantly, we have factual information on your current climate—and upcoming changes to same. You are not a dumb politician, Premier. I know that you have had the same climate forecasts done as we have.

"I know that the changes will mean that the global warming is only a slight issue but that the rise in sea levels—especially for your huge island resort industry—will be a problem. You know it's going to mean, in some cases, total island flooding and loss of the major part of the Bottle tourist industry," she said.

She stopped, took a long pull of her iced tea, and smiled at him. "Your ice caps are melting at a rapid pace. No one knows why, but I suspect that your scientists have some interesting ideas on your sun and its output perhaps. More than we have, but that's not important. Your oceans will rise. And the rise in sea level is estimated to be at least four feet and as much as nine feet. Small numbers, it's true, but it would mean that most island resorts—yes, our own too, will be underwater. Bottle is changing, Premier, we know it. You know it. But we offer a hand out to the planet, if you'd consider this," she said.

He gulped some iced tea and just stared at her.

"Bottle will join the Barony with full realm member privileges. You will retain the premiership for at least, say, ten years as my own contact here. We will, with our newfound riches from our Barony Drive and our Ikarian longevity vaccine, fully support the Bottle economy and bypass any economic catastrophe that you might face. Nothing else will change, Premier—if we help your planet to survive ..." she said, and she leaned back to sip her iced tea again.

He fiddled with his straw in the tall frosted glass and said nothing for a full five minutes. While she wasn't sure yet about which way he'd jump, she did see that he knew the economic catastrophe would cost him his premiership for sure. He knew that. What she'd offered was a way out.

"Full membership? Realm status? Seat at the RIM Confederacy Council behind you?" he asked.

Done, she thought, and she smiled broadly at him and laid a gentle hand on his forearm. "Guaranteed, Premier. Welcome to the Barony, and I'll have my people get in touch soon to get the paperwork started. Now, what's good here for lunch?" she said.

He blinked at her and almost stuttered as he reached for a menu and tried to move on.

The Barony has just grown by one more planet— we're now eleven and closing on the Alex'n hegemony ... with the duchy to be added soon, she thought. I will soon be RIM Confederacy Council chairperson ... not too shabby. She smiled as she listened to the premier talk about salads and other menu items he'd recommend.

Taking the *Sword* up to the Hospital Ship had been an uneventful trip, but as Tanner looked out the window from his seat on the starboard side of the cockpit, he realized quickly that he missed space.

The emptiness of the blackness out here on the RIM was one thing, but that made the much fewer stars that he could see all that more important. The giant band of the galaxy was off to his far right, and he always enjoyed seeing that, yet being here on the RIM was somehow better. Somehow more fulfilling, he thought, and as he realized he was starting to reflect more than he wanted to, he snorted out loud, and beside him, his pilot, Lieutenant Cooper, started.

"Sir, all okay?" he asked.

"Roger that, Lieutenant—just thinking on something else," he said as he shook his head.

No sense in waxing philosophically, he thought as he watched his pilot pivot the *Sword* so gracefully to port, enter the enormous landing bay, and taxi up to the lit-up landing space reserved for them.

"Back in a bit, Lieutenant, but you've time for lunch if you'd like. Try the CPR Café up on Deck C, near the far left end of the main corridor. It is about the best on the ship," he added as he left the cockpit of the *Sword*, moved down the main corridor to the landing ramp, as it now jutted out, and walked down the ramp.

He grinned right away at Maddie and gave her a big hug, and she squirmed a bit as he did that.

"Lord Scott, that's not right, My Lord ... you are Royalty and Royalty—"

"Never gets a chance to be personal, I know, I know, Maddie. But I have missed you and wanted to just say hi!" he said.

The blush on her face meant much to him, and she looked down at her shoes as she was embarrassed by his display of obvious affection. Their relationship had been pretty intense back some time ago, and she was more than aware that here in the landing port, others might have seen his hug. And while that didn't worry her at all for herself, she was worried about what it might look like to others on his behalf.

He grinned at her, took her arm, and led her away from the ship.

"Maddie, Maddie. Always worrying about

others. Let me tell you that the life of a Royal is not at all what it's cracked up to be ... but I would admit that I no longer have to wait in line for anything anymore."

She nodded and as they walked inward, she was careful to keep a bit removed from him and his hugging arm.

He realized that after a few steps and let go of her, and they both headed toward the landing port doors ahead of them. Moving along, they made their way to the moving walkway and stepped on it to travel to the center axis of the ship.

"Maddie, what is new here?" he inquired politely.

She cocked her head and looked at him. "Do you mean medicine-wise or ... people-wise ... or patient-wise, My Lord?"

He grinned at her. "Please, drop the My Lord title—to you I'm always just going to be Tanner, okay?"

"Not okay, My Lord. A part of being a Royal is the understanding that you're different than us commoners, so I just can't do that—My Lord," she said as she shook her head at him.

He sighed. What she said was most likely true, and that was a sad fact he'd have to go along with.

"Patient-wise—and I'm concerned, of course, about one special patient," he said as the walkway slowly moved up to the central axis with its escalators going up and down. From here, one could go anywhere on the ship—well, except for the secure labs areas, but still it gave access to almost everywhere else.

Maddie nodded as she stepped on the up escalator on their way to see Doctor Etter. "She checked into room E-217—your old room—as per instructions. She has Doctor Etter as her personal psychiatrist and attends group sessions under Doctor Lathan Trystan—again, same as you. She has been with us now for about ninety days or so, and all I can tell you is what I've seen to be true. She's a nice young woman. Of course, she's a murderer, and one can never forget that either, but she is fitting in nicely. I hear good things from Doctor Trystan too, about her group work—make sure you ask about that too, Tann—My Lord," she said. She'd almost slipped but had caught herself.

Tanner nodded at the information she'd just given him. Fitting in. Nice was a word that had been used by Maddie—someone he trusted implicitly. Of course, she'd also said murderer too, and that too was true.

He didn't smile. He didn't do anything except look up ahead as the escalator reached the first floor above the Hospital Ship lobby level. He and Maddie turned to go to D-198, Doctor Etter's offices. As they walked, he noted the absolute cleanliness of the ship's corridors, doors, and rooms that he could peer into as they walked along. Out in the hallway, there were often some stored items like a crash cart or a gurney, and he could see not a speck of dirt or dust or anything at all. Clean. Neat. And ready for use, he thought as Maddie opened up the outer door and they went inside Doctor Etter's offices.

The receptionist, a new one, he noted, smiled at them and waved them in as the inner door opened up, and Doctor Trystan greeted them first. Tanner knew the doctor had been a great help to him when he was here, and while he'd learned a bit from Maddie, he still took the doctor's hand and pumped it vigorously. He did the same as Doctor Etter rose from behind his desk and came around to greet Tanner.

Hell with it, Tanner thought, and he hugged the psychiatrist and got a solid hug back. He grinned at him and said, "Sam, so nice to see you once again," and he meant it too.

Sam grinned back at him and motioned for him to take a seat. They settled in, with Maddie on his left and Doctor Trystan to his right. On the other side of the desk, Doctor Etter got himself comfortable and opened up both his hands, palms up as he spoke.

"My Lord—so good to see you up and around. I followed your rest and recuperation quite closely—the Lady St. August was kind enough to keep me informed, and I concurred with every single bit of care that you received. You look hale and hearty, My Lord," he said. "More than a few months have passed since the wedding and the murders, and that you are here and alive is the best news of all," he added.

Everyone nodded and turned to look at Tanner.

"I thank you all—and Doctor Etter—for my life too, really … you were right there on the spot seconds after the shots, and if it had not been for you and your medical care immediately, I too might not be present, like my friends the Duke d'Avigdor and the Master Adept," he said. His voice was solemn; it was a simple fact that Doctor Etter had saved his life.

"My Lord—there was a full complement of trained medical personnel only a few feet away, and the robo-doc was wheeled up to you in less than five minutes. I did what any doctor would have done is all—they took it from there," he said.

Tanner smiled. "Yes, but those first few minutes were critical, Doctor—for that, I thank you," he said, and the man across the desk from him bowed his head.

Tanner sat back and took a second to look

around. The office was exactly as he remembered it. Bland. No style or substance, but beige walls. He grinned to himself. The person facing the psychiatrist should be the focus of the room, rather than artwork on the walls or tchotchkes on the bookcase, was the real rationale for the bland room. He wondered if the good doctor still kept his own weapon up on the top shelf in that wooden box, but that query would need to wait.

He moved on to the reason he'd made the trip to the Hospital Ship.

"Doctors," he said to the two of them in the room, "I came as it's just about ninety days that Gia Scott has been a patient here—and I'd like an update on what you have found out so far.

"As I understand our Barony privacy laws, such information would be hidden to one and all—but I ask as a Royal, which I'm told forgoes any such restrictions. Plus, as you both know, she is my sister —so I'm officially next of kin for sure."

He'd paid attention to his wife when he'd asked for that breakdown of what he could and couldn't ask for—and the fact that he was Lord Scott outweighed any issues at all.

Doctor Trystan cleared his throat to speak. "Lord Scott—damn, it feels funny saying that, but I must. Gia is within our group session roster and is doing surprisingly well—at least that's my unofficial diagnosis. She both listens and speaks her mind; she is a strong woman. She gives out praise and often commiserates with others too—she is a compassionate patient with others. She has offered up some looks 'inside' her own way of thinking that, at least to start with, show me that there are a few things in her life that for her—they're carved in stone.

"One of those, sorry to say, is her hatred for you. I have not explored that to any degree, but instead, as is the rule with group sessions, I've let her bring it out herself. So far, she has been mostly guarded about the reason for the hatred and her sister's death—but she is quite open about how much she despises you—backed up, she has let slip a few times, by what her mother—your mother—told her."

Lathan's voice was serious, and yet to Tanner, he heard a tone that sounded cautiously optimistic. It was a bit of information that he could dwell on later.

Doctor Etter chimed in then too. "And I concur on all of that. We've had many discussions about Gia, and as you've undoubtedly guessed, we think there may be a way to help her. As Doctor Trystan said, the ingrained instinctual hatred of you comes from your mother—at least so far, that is our diagnosis.

"In our individual sessions, she has proclaimed that she loved her sister, that she was torn from her life by you—and that you did that all because you were trying to 'earn your wings,' as she put it, with your planetary space program.

"At this point, My Lord, she has not yet identified her mother as the culprit—but that, I think, is coming. Once we can get her to see that her mother was, and is, the cause of her hatred for you, perhaps then we can begin to make some inroads on how she can give up that thinking."

"And I'd also like to thank you for that in-depth report that you sent us about the death of your sister. It will help us both in the future to combat those 'carved in stone' opinions about her avenging her sister, Nora, by killing the man that had killed her, Tanner Scott. The fact that he was her brother meant nothing to her," Doctor Etter said, looking pointedly at Tanner.

Tanner took a deep breath and leaned back in his chair.

Doctor Etter continued. "The fact that the Branton courts had found him guiltless in Nora's death meant nothing. The fact that her mother had known that Tanner had sacrificed Nora meant everything ..."

The room was silent, and Tanner nodded.

As he had suspected, she held a hate for him that

was deep-set and rooted into her psyche by his mother. He felt little for the woman who had given birth to him — at least after the death of Nora. And the fact she had passed along her hatred of him to his only remaining sister meant much more.

If he would ever have a chance to converse with Gia, she would need to be more receptive than the current state of her mind with regards to him.

He nodded once more. "Doctor Etter and Doctor Trystan — can I ask this? About how long should I wait before coming back for more news — failing a breakthrough of some type, I mean?" he asked.

Doctor Etter smiled at him and pushed his hand across his desk. "My Lord, at least, say, another three months or so? If there are any unexpected changes in the patient, we will immediately get in touch — after all, as you've said, you are the next of kin.

"We can reconvene in ninety days and talk more. Not promising that there will be anything more to discuss, but she is making some progress, My Lord," he said as he slowly rose behind his desk.

Minutes later, on the down escalator, Maddie, who was accompanying him back to the *Sword*, interrupted his silence.

"My Lord, I'm sure that there will be some progress made. She already is looking around and thinking that this could be her home forevermore —

and I'm just as sure she knows that she will need to make some changes to her psyche to be able to move on ... least as far as I can figure it," she said.

He nodded to her and moments later, the *Sword* slipped out of the Hospital Ship on its way back to the Neres City naval base and home.

CHAPTER SEVEN

Court at the Teuku palace was as it might be expected — pompous yet, for some reason, a tad less so than what one might imagine. The big, sandstone building had ceilings that were exceptionally high and wide, wide corridors and rooms, but it somehow seemed warm to the Entiran as he walked down the third floor hallway to the major intersection ahead.

There, he turned to his left and nodded at the aides who had awaited his presence and now trooped ahead of him toward the presentation room. As he walked slowly and the aides matched his own slower speed, he saw old paintings on the wall that showed women, and he grinned.

Women, even in paintings, should be banned as well, he thought, and he decided this was something for the new Tillion Narrisol—him—to accomplish!

He entered the room from a side door, as he always did, took the four steps up to the dais at the end of the room, quickly sat in the Entiran throne, and got comfortable—or at least he tried. The large ornate chair was hundreds of years old, but the designer had not taken into account that as time went on, an Entiran would become more of an administrator and less of a noble chieftain.

The chair was too narrow for him, and he thought about telling an aide to widen it—but then again, there was a traditional sense of not altering what came before you when you were born into the nobility of his tribe. Instead, one was taught to conform to the previous historical profiles of those who had sat in this throne before him.

The tribe's colors of red and white were a major feature in his courtly attire today. Today's was his second favorite, and when he'd dressed for the court session earlier, he took notice of how nicely the wide red brim jutted out from his scalp. His boots were bright white Jael leather with red buckles and ties up the outsides. He loved his boots even though they didn't look like the boots of a nation's leader.

He nodded to an aide to his left and leaned back, his hips constrained by the hard wooden frame of the seat; there was little space for comfort in the wooden seat. He wondered if the seat was intentionally made narrow to ensure each Entiran made a quick decision and moved on—and quickly up and out of the throne as the citizen presentations were done.

He watched the double doors open and a small group of his ministers walked toward him. Four. There were four of them, yet there was really only one of them—the Minister of Trade—and he was an ally for the tribe, the Entiran thought as he let a very tiny smile appear on his face, and he nodded to the man.

His group was well dressed, of course, as was the tradition when one went to court to see their leader. He had to admit that he rather liked the green shade of sable that was on one of their hats. Must find out that color, he thought, and see what I can do to acquire something in that shade too.

"Entiran, we greet you and wish to say our thanks for the time you give us today," the minister up front said quietly and calmly.

He nodded and waved at the man, ensuring his middle eyebrow stayed in line with the other two. No sense in telegraphing any kind of interest yet, he thought.

The minister went on. "We were under instructions to begin to use our own ministry to see what we might be able to accomplish with the uni-gender issue that all of Tillion faces. We listened to your instructions carefully, and yes, you were, of course, as correct as all the Entirans before you were as well.

"We have no women of our species. We use our technology to supplement our numbers, and that is something that all of Tillion has been—at the least —hiding from the RIM Confederacy.

"We, unlike the rest of the planet, want to bring this information out—not by a blast that ripples throughout the Confederacy, but more like a grassroots citizens cause,as you called it, Entiran," he said. He held out his hand, and from behind him, one of his aides handed him a folder of documents. He took a half step ahead and was met by one of the court aides, who took the folder and carried it up to the throne.

Taking for a minute or two to read over same, the Entiran smiled, his third eyebrow arching up in a smooth arc, and he closed the folder and passed it back to his aide, who returned it to the minister. "I see, minister, that you've been able to use your own ministry to um ... gently, let us say, get some kind of a student gathering conference together at the university, just a week ago. I also see that the speakers were, let us say, very vocal about the uni-gender issue and how it was time to open up to the

Confederacy about same.

"I also see that the university campus police were not so understanding and that there were some minor altercations as they attempted to close down the conference. The Press reported on same, but as I remember, only barely and not fully either. That meant that there were, and are now, some students who feel that their opinions are being censored," he said.

The Entiran stopped speaking and looked at the group before him. Taking a breath, he continued, "While we all know that students can't get much done—we need, I believe, to somehow nurture follow-ups to this conference. Perhaps you might get the faculty involved—have them try to squelch any more of same, to egg the students on to increase their voices and their newly found pressure on the university. I must congratulate you as to how you have launched this so quickly; the students believe they are simply voicing what is real to them, but the import is to get this blown up and big even more quickly, Minister. How will you achieve that?" he asked.

The minister's eyebrows, all three of them, reached up well toward the brim of his own hat as he smiled fully to his Entiran. "We think that, yes, we will instill in our student agitators that they invade the next university faculty board meeting and take it over—a sort of sit-in to force the uni-gender issue to the board. This will undoubtedly be forcefully resisted by the campus police, and we will ensure that some students pay a big price, violence-wise to blow this up. That should—as we intend to get some of our press contacts into that meeting as well—get the uni-gender issue up and on the planetary news feeds," he said.

The Entiran nodded. National press news would mean a messy scandal of massive proportions. Such a mess would not be swept under the rug by the Narrisol and his cabinet but instead challenge them at their most vulnerable level.

"And the new birthing lab video captures?" he asked.

One of the group in front of him nodded, and more discussion ensued about how that was to be played by the students who would receive it as a "brown envelope" donation from someone in the birthing labs who had a mission to publicize same. It was believed someone in the labs was on their side.

It had taken almost two months, but a new hire at those labs was a citizen from the Duchy d'Avigdor. He was a scientist who had already been somewhat tarnished for his left-wing leanings on Dover, a planet with major pharmaceutical industry, and he'd needed a new job. The Entiran smiled at what had come to them so quickly, and that third eyebrow settled slowly.

All things were coming together, except for this damned narrow seat, the Entiran thought as he squirmed to his left a bit more.

"Let some of your contacts in the press in on that brown-bag whistle-blower—not the contents at this point, I'd think, but that there is growing support for the uni-gender publicizing of same ..." he said and smiled.

It had proven true that the Caliph would provide the impetus.

But the next Narrisol of Tillion at in this uncomfortable throne—a sign he hoped was not foretelling his future.

#####

Not being assigned to a current ship has its bonuses, Bram thought as he walked down the landing ramp of the BN Coventry. The frigate had just landed at Odonje, the planetary capital on Throth. The ship had arrived from Turljis, and Bram was hoping this trip to Throth would be productive. It'd been weeks since he'd been asked by the Master Adept to find more Praix planets here in the RIM Confederacy, and as yet, he was unsuccessful.

As he nodded to the Provost guard at the gate to

the administration building, he smiled at the man and wondered whom he'd pissed off to get such a poor posting—then he realized that such was not the case at all. Throth was a positive posting, he realized, as he looked around the street in front of where he stood.

Big wide city street. No traffic. Not a single car or truck or even a wagon with an Ikarian at the reins and the taulevs pulling the cart.

Above the buildings ahead and a distance away, he could see a few cranes used in construction, but here, close to the Throth landing port, there was none of the traffic that such construction was usually accompanied by.

Even though there were some shops that looked open, he didn't see a single Ikarian in sight. Near the shops was a café with a patio, but it had empty tables and chairs.

"If you're a Provost guard, who looks after community safety and enforces the law, having no one around is a good thing," he said to himself as he opened the door to the administration building.

Ah, here are all the people! he thought. Aliens, actually, he reminded himself, and his mind began to open up to what was before him. A human janitor appeared to be polishing a floor on one side of the big lobby, and behind the reception desk was an Ikarian—a child—who looked up at him.

Her mind was wide open, and he smiled to himself when he saw she was eagerly awaiting her lunch break because there were two cupcakes in her lunch bag that she was waiting patiently for.

"May I help you, Lieutenant?" she inquired with a voice that was more mature than her early teenage years.

He smiled at her. Her black hair and her bright, bright blue eyes shone up at him as he noted her plain yet nicely pressed jerkin top, its leather and fringe all neat and tidy.

"Yes, you may, young lady. I would like to see the administrator if I could? RIM Confederacy business is the reason, and I'm a bit pressed for time," he said.

She looked down at the console in front of her, and after a few keyboard clicks, she looked up at him and then back down at the console. She clicked some more keys, and then she looked up at him again.

"But Lieutenant, your ship, the BN Coventry, is just starting a refill on the anti-matter, which will take at the quickest more than two hours, Sir," she said. In her mind, Bram saw this simple fact had her stumped as to why he was in a hurry, so she'd asked.

Guess there is little to be gained by pressuring a receptionist, he thought, but he was glad that her mind, like most youngsters' minds, was wide open to his Issian powers.

He nodded. "Yes, I meant that I'd like to speak to the administrator as soon as you can arrange that— and I apologize for not arranging this meeting ahead of time. If the admin can even spare a half hour, that'd be all I need," he said nicely.

She nodded back to him, and the tapping sound of her keyboard keys filled the air. She smiled up at him. "Sir, yes, Ahanu can meet with you—I'm to send you up right away. Please take the left staircase up three floors, and then on the third floor, head left to the second door on your left, Sir," she said, and she smiled as the thoughts of those cupcakes came back into the forefront of her mind.

He nodded and walked to the staircase on the left to climb to the third floor. Coming out of the staircase on the third floor, he turned to his left and went down the hallway to the second door on his left.

ADMIN was printed on the door, and he smiled as he entered. As he walked toward the secretary, the inner door opened and out came Ahanu—his friend.

They grinned at each other, and Ahanu gave the traditional Ikarian sign of respect—the back of his right hand, pressed against his forehead and held there for some seconds. Bram followed suit, and they grinned at each other for several seconds and then clasped each other in a hug.

"Bram. So good of you to drop by, and it's been too long," Ahanu said as he turned to lead his friend into his office.

Bram smiled back and said, "Yes, and under better circumstances too, Ahanu ..."

The last time they had seen each other was at Lord Scott's wedding. Both had been ushers in the ceremony, and both had seen the assassination of the Master Adept and the duke, as well as the shooting of Lord Scott. It had been a solemn and terrible time for them both, but that was in the past.

Ahanu's smile was replaced with a look of regret for a moment, and Bram could see in his mind that he was sorry he'd even mentioned that it'd been a long time since they'd been together.

Bram gently squeezed Ahanu's arm and smiled. "Not to worry—but tell me, what is it like to go from a sleeper ship crewman to being the admin for a whole planet?" he said as he took his seat in front of the desk.

Ahanu walked around the desk to sit behind it. The office held the desk, some chairs out front, and an enormous floor-to-ceiling window on one side that looked out to the big landing port. There, Bram could see the chandlers fitting the Coventry with new supplies and the big red anti-grav fill truck as the work went on.

Ahanu smiled. Under his jet-black brows, his big Ikarian blue eyes shone at his friend. Dressed today in soft light brown buckskin, or quollskin, he looked more like a real live warrior than a planetary administrator as he sat perched on the office chair beneath him.

"It is what you humans call 'boring' at times, yet somehow all the little pieces and odds and ends that make up each day do come together and make for a sense of 'well done' at times. Other times, I pull out what little hair I have left," he said.

On his head, of course, lay the coal-black long locks of an adult Ikarian. He'd kept the braids down his back, and they were long and well kept. He was joking, Bram realized, about the hair thing, but he knew the sheer number of small items that needed a look-see by the planetary administrator was probably more than he'd like to see at all.

"Delegate, Ahanu … delegate! And learn to find better people to handle the details," he said.

Ahanu nodded and answered with a rueful face. "But as we Ikarians have more than ten thousand children in our care and less than a thousand adults, the number of adults that I can acquire to help govern is very much limited. We also, of course, hire humans and other Confederacy citizens to help, but the thrill of coming to Throth to work seems to be somewhat limited," he said.

Bram nodded. It was true that a job was a job, but without some kind of bonus, off-planet hiring was going to be a tough row to hoe.

After a half hour of small talk, Bram turned the talk to the reason for his trip to Throth.

"Ahanu, yes, I'll provide some full docs on the Barony pioneer program and how it got Ghayth more than three hundred thousand new citizens in less than a year. Perhaps taking that program and adapting it to your own use could help. But let me tell you why I'm here today," he said.

Ahanu's mind was not registering any kind of quandary, and so Bram went ahead.

"I am looking for evidence of previous alien— ancient alien—visitations to our Barony worlds," he said right up front.

Ahanu said nothing, and Bram noted a big question mark filling his mind.

"We want to know if any of our worlds have been visited by aliens in the last, say, twenty thousand years. I know that this is somewhat difficult to understand even, but it's from the top, and all I want to know is this, Ahanu. If you find any such evidence—old ruins or secret warehouses or ruined technology—let me know? We think that there were some visitations about two hundred centuries ago, and we're looking to vet what we already know. So my job is to go out to our own Barony planets and ask. Just came from Turljis, and there was nothing there. But like them, if you keep that in mind and something does come up, just let me know?" he asked.

The quest was for the Issians—the Master Adept in fact—rather than the Barony, but it posed little problem for Bram. The evidence of such a visitation would be of interest to both—and he could claim he was just showing some initiative based on his knowledge of Ghayth. As the Master Adept had advised, this was a great cover, and for his own part, it posed no problems for him, integrity-wise. He was doing both realms a favor, and that was that.

Ahanu still had nothing that jumped out to the forefront of his brain. None of the other Barony planet administrators had either. Bram's method was to ask a question on a particular topic, and then read their mind for what jumped out—or what was trying to be hidden as some attempted. He could change the question based on the information he was looking for, but his method still worked, and it always worked even if someone tried to hide their knowledge.

Ahanu nodded to him and held up a hand, palm up. "I know nothing of this, Bram, but will pay attention should this ever come up. We know—

well, most of the Barony planets know—that something is "up" over on Ghayth—and I hope that if we can help, we shall," he said.

"And a gentle reminder, Ahanu? That this is a confidential search ... please keep it 'close to your vest,' as we say out here on the RIM."

Ahanu's head tilted to one side. Moments later, he smiled and nodded. "Ah, got it, Bram. Good to know that one too—and yes, I'll keep it 'under wraps,' as you also sometimes say too."

They both smiled at each other. A pact, Bram thought, that we both can honor, and he nodded to Ahanu and rose all in one motion.

"Ahanu, as always, good to see you, and may your planet do well under your guidance," he said grandly.

Ahanu rose too and once again offered up the Ikarian sign of respect before walking toward the office door. Bram followed, and they both walked out to the outer office.

The secretary had returned, and the young man was sitting at his desk and rose as well. Well mannered, Bram thought, as he scanned the youngster's mind. He didn't find much except for a question about who the Issian visiting Ahanu was.

He smiled at the youngster. "So that you might know for the future," he said to the boy, "I am Lieutenant Bram Sander, of the Barony Navy, and

I'm an old friend of your administrator's. Just here to catch up is all, but I will be back. Perhaps, if the time is right, we might go quoll hunting ... I think I might like that," he added.

Thinking about quoll hunting brought up Bram's memory of Lord Scott's run-in with quoll. Tanner had been severely injured as a quoll had attacked him and had taken both Tanner and his taulev to the ground. Bram didn't think he had better than average hunting skills. Well, at least I think I could try, he thought, but Ahanu was already motioning to his secretary.

"Norbert—line that up with my upcoming vacation time and work out the details. Let Lieutenant Sander here know about what dates might be available, and yes, Bram, let's go hunting," he said with great enthusiasm and a huge smile.

Now I've done it, Bram thought as he slowly took the stairs back down to the lobby and then across the still empty street to the landing port gate. Hope I can bring a laser ...

#####

As she walked, she realized that she hadn't been in this area of Dessau before. The narrow streets—some she too narrow to hold a robo-cab — surrounded her. She walked down the narrow street and past tall, three-story homes, some with overhangs above her head. Behind her, two of her aides walked along, not so much following as leading. Even though she was in the front, each time she'd tried to head back to the more populated streets to her right, she'd gotten a hint from behind that she should instead turn to her left.

Now, after more than an hour of walking, talking to Issian citizens, and offering up the truly kind words of a Master Adept, she suddenly knew why she was being herded this way.

Ahead of her, as she turned to the left yet again, was a small park with a child's playground with swings and teeter-totters. From a ring of small flagpoles around the playground, Issian flags with the ringed planet flew. In today's light winds, they fluttered, and some even snapped too.

Park benches ran around the outside of the small green space, and most were filled with moms and their children. As her mind reached out, it recoiled back.

These were the Mournfuls.

These Issians had received the genes that would make them able to read minds—superb genes to be truthful, she thought—but they had not received much else from the Issian gene pool. The Mournfuls were born with what could only be called less than normal intelligence. Despite others trying to teach

213

them—repeatedly—these Issians did not know how to do things like feed themselves, clothe themselves, talk, or sing. Sadly, the Mournfuls were unable to do much at all.

Her eyes filled with tears immediately, and she slowly advanced on the closest park bench to sit cautiously near a mom who held a small boy on her lap. Blond, of course, most Mournfuls were born with blond hair. He paid no attention to her but stared straight ahead while his mother continued to slowly stroke his arm. But as she tilted her head toward the Master Adept, her eyes locked onto hers.

She dabbed at her left eye, and the tear was quickly wiped away. She pushed her sorrow for the mother and her family out with her mind.

The mother dipped her head as an answer, and a small smile appeared on her face. "We thank the Master Adept, and we hope that she comes here often. Many here would like to just say hello ... we Mournfuls, as you might realize, are Issians too," she said quietly.

The Master Adept nodded and asked if her boy was okay—she had no other word to use, she realized.

The mother nodded. "As well as any boy might be—except his mind is not here in the park with us. Where it might be, we all do not know, but he is a good boy, nonetheless," she said positively and smiled.

Proud of her son like any mother, the Master Adept thought.

"Yes, I am the new Master Adept, and if you ever, ever need anything—any of you here in the park—you simply come to the walled city and ask for me. Anytime. Day or night—and for any reason," she said, and she meant it.

She rose and sat with some of the others in the park. She'd asked one why the park seemed to draw the Mournfuls to it—as she had seen the children were too fragile to ever use the playground rides and games. That mother had said she had no idea; it was just where they went. Another later on had said maybe the flapping of the flags made the child Mournfuls quiet as they often sat and stared at the flags. Another asked where else were they to go; she said this was their exile from Dessau.

That gave Gloria an idea, and she filed it away for later. She spent almost two hours there, talking to every single mother and noticing all the blond heads that seemed to be mesmerized by the flapping ringed planet flags, bright blue on an orange background.

As she rose from the final bench, she nodded to her aides who had simply followed her from bench to bench. She said, "Let's go back," and she led the

215

way out of the park and back toward the more populated area of the city near the core.

As she led the way, her thoughts were already moving off the Mournfuls she'd just been introduced to, and she thought more about the whole RIM Confederacy instead.

She knew, as all did, that the new short list to merge with the Duchy d'Avigdor, was the Caliphate and the Barony. She also knew, as few did, that the dukedom had been offered to Lord Scott, who, it appeared, was not going to accept. That meant that the new power that was to be here on the web, might be hers to enable.

She knew that the Caliphate—the Caliph more than the realm—was not friendly with the Issians and Eons. She knew that the Barony, however, had seen "eye to eye" between the Baroness and the previous Master Adept.

She knew that should the Barony get the Duchy d'Avigdor, it'd then have the most number of planets in their realm, which would mean the Baroness would succeed to the chairman's title of the RIM Confederacy—something she wanted.

And helping the Baroness to succeed would make the Baroness very, very happy as well as in the debt of the Issians.

"Really not much to think about," she said to herself as she turned the final corner, and the streets ahead opened up greatly. As she strode now with a degree of purpose back toward the waiting row of robo-cabs, she realized she'd just made up her mind —and the Issian mind too—her rationale being the reason that she'd been made the new Master Adept. She smiled.

She dipped a shoulder to take the rear seat of the robo-cab, and after waiting for her aides to get into the front, she spoke to them for the first time today.

"When we get back to my quarters, I want an EYES ONLY scheduled with the Baroness of Neres ASAP," she said.

Both aides in the seat in front of her nodded.

"I also want to create something for the Mournfuls. A new park—a full-sized park with real grass and park benches like the one we were just in. But I want more flags and the like—things that move—maybe some kind of an animated children's entertainment center—puppets or animatronics or the like.

"Have someone check with the Eons University on Mournfuls too—how can we make life for them easier. Better. Simpler. And yet not—and I do not, I repeat not, want a charity feel to any of this—hear me?" she said, her voice now as hard as steel.

"Yes, Ma'am," the two aides said in unison.

"I also want Bram. Get him here as soon as he's able, I have more for him to do. And schedule a mind merge session for later tonight as well—the inner circle only, of course", she said.

"Get it done," she finished, and the nods from the front went on for some time.

"Final product test number RX-117, at twenty-five thousand kelvins," the lab scientist in the white coat said as the lab AI began to record the testing.

In the chamber before him, protected by more than twenty inches of solid pure titanium held in the most powerful force field the Leudies could find, the man stood stock-still bathed in the glow of the power belt that was being tested. So far, a simple blast of the most powerful laser out on the RIM at seventeen hundred kelvins had not penetrated the belt, and the man had lived. He'd also lived through all the projectile tests using everything from bows and arrows to bullets and even mortars and cannons too. He'd lived through all the energy weapons as well, from lasers to energy pulse weapons and plasma ship cannons. "Getting the damn equipment down here had been a real chore," the scientist said as he shrugged, but the belt had kept the man alive.

Now simple heat testing was the final set of tests. The temperature of a star ran from about five thousand kelvins up to about twenty thousand

kelvins at the top end. The man was still standing
after tests at six thousand kelvins, twelve thousand
kelvins, and twenty thousand kelvins, fired at him
by the energy pulse cannon built into the testing
chamber. Now, for the final test of twenty-five
thousand kelvins, and if the man still stood—alive
—then the power belt was truly an invulnerable
shield to anything that man, alien, or any creature
could throw at it.

The scientist dialed up the final test on the
console of the unit in front of him and smiled.
Wearing such a belt would eliminate every single
method that would harm the wearer. Wearing such
a belt would make the wearer a true super-being.

Of course, it also, he knew, cut the wearer off
from all contact with others around him or her.
While you were safe, you were isolated, and that
would mean that, for some at least, it was a
singularly solitary existence.

He looked at the man inside the chamber via the
camera, flashed the lights inside the required three
times, counted to three, and then hit the big red
button to have the energy pulse cannon shoot the
full twenty-five-thousand-kelvin blast at the man.

As usual, the chamber AI closed all contact
between the inside of the chamber and the scientist
who stood outside watching. Still, there was a feel,
he thought, to that much power being expended

within feet of where he stood, and it may have been just an unconscious thought, but he flinched.

As his eyes opened, he waited until the camera was re-inserted back into the chamber, turned on, focused, and yes ... there stood the man.

Alive.

Alone.

But alive ... and he smiled while for the AI, he said slowly and succinctly, "Final test RX-117, of twenty-five thousand kelvins, proved the belt continued to be up and running fine. No effects to the test subject. And at eighteen thousand kelvins, that's the same temperature as, say, Rigel inwards but yet well known. With this test, we conclude the testing cycle and acknowledge that the power belt is truly invincible.

"Test closed. File closed. Send file over to Factor, the capital city on Leudie, directly to the attention of the Rulers themselves under the official, if unused, name, the Leudie Trading Rules Group."

They'd been testing this imported product for more than a year now, and now that the actual testing on live subjects had been completed, there was only one thing left to do. Find more and export them to the RIM Confederacy.

He smiled as he tucked his stylo into the large pocket protector in his lab coat's breast pocket. It was time to let the RIM know that anyone who

could afford one would be a god here on the RIM.
This would be a tremendous revenue generator for
the Leudi Rulers.

CHAPTER EIGHT

For a lieutenant in the Barony Navy, this trip up
to the Hospital Ship was more, Bram thought, than
he wanted to be made public. Bram needed to be
careful since he was there in different capacities for
different reasons.

He was there to find out if there was anything
new to learn about Gia and her mental state. He
was also interested to know what he could find out
from the medical team handling her case; he was
sure that reading their minds would reveal
additional information.

Any information he uncovered would have to be
shared with two people, even if he kept some things
back. His Master Adept expected him to be her
mole within the Barony Navy and report his
findings about Gia to her. If Lord Scott found out

about his visit, he would expect Bram to share information about Gia with him. Bram had a close friendship with Tanner, and all of the machinations were weighing heavily on his conscience.

"Add to that," he said to himself, "is the fact that I am hopelessly attracted to this beautiful assassin too, and that makes the whole position more than a hardship—it makes it all so surreal."

He felt like he should—he must—be here to speak to Doctor Etter to try to solve some of the issues he faced. Yet he also thought he should have stayed on Throth with Ahanu and just gone hunting. The Throth quolls were now fully grown, and the hunting trip carried the risk of serious injury or even death, but when he weighed that against what he faced on the Hospital Ship, it seemed like an easier and better choice.

"Fat chance," he said to himself as he walked down the landing ramp off the shuttle and moved along with the flow of other passengers to the moving walkway ahead. He took advantage of the well-posted directional signs, and as the walkway delivered him in the main ship's huge towering lobby, he stepped off.

Calling ahead had gotten him an appointment with Doctor Etter, Gia's psychiatrist. Since he was almost an hour early, he walked over to a seating bench along the one wall and watched the crowd of people around him.

Medical folks, he saw, still wore white generally, as every lab coat and short jacket was white, but they also wore scrubs. All the medical people he saw wore scrubs with matching light pastel-colored tops and bottoms. Almost all wore some kind of rubber or synthetic-soled shoes that gave great purchase on the metal deck plates. Almost all had, from the few dozen he'd seen at least, short hair with no real wild colorations—though a couple of Tillion medical people still wore those wide-brimmed hats.

Over to his left was a juice bar had a line waiting to order, and he was noting those folks when his eyes froze. Gia was next in line to order.

He slightly turned in his seat to look at her a bit closer, and he tried to make sure nobody, especially Gia, could tell he was staring at her. Her hair was cut off at her jawline and was a collection of light brown and blonde locks. Her back was straight, but she had an ability to look like she was flexed and ready to jump at any second—maybe he imagined that, he thought.

She looked like she was an athlete as she took those few steps forward to order her juice. She looked balanced and lithe, supple yet nimble, somehow after just those couple of steps. He couldn't hear what she ordered, but moments later, she walked away with a large dark-cerise-colored juice drink. She walked away from him, but then she dropped into another bench on the opposite side of his and sipped away at the drink, lost in thought it appeared to him.

He sat and hid his glances at her, but he watched nonetheless. She sucked away at the straw, and the juice must have been a thick drink as she continued to suck heartily at it. She was wearing scrubs too, he just noticed, in a pale sea green color, and her shoes were sneakers. She wore the arm bracelet that all patients wore, and while it was too far away for him to read anything on it, he saw the color was bright neon blue. One hand was twisting a strand of her hair while the other supported the juice drink. One leg was crossed over the other, and she bounced that foot up in the air over and over.

She looked, Bram thought, as if she had not a care in the world. And he reached out with his mind to see what he might find.

He jolted back slightly, as the turmoil of what he saw in her head was a surprise. She was upset and feeling so righteous that she was broadcasting that state of mind forcefully. Not via her body or any outward signs, but her brain was going a mile a minute as she asked herself question after question, and Bram could easily see same.

Why did Tanner kill Nora?

Why did Doctor Etter say no, that didn't happen?

How could the Branton government get to the doctor to poison his mind so that he would say that?

Why had Mom been so sure—Doctor Etter said she was wrong, but why?

Who else might be here on the ship that she should be afraid of?

Where could she run to for safety?

Why did Doctor Etter think that he was right and my Mom was wrong?

The thoughts were all jumbled together with no real pause between any of them. She went over and over the same questions, and they never stopped as they ran through her brain.

Bram wondered for a moment if he should enter the conversation and insert an answer, or even two, to some of those questions, but then he remembered that Doctor Etter was one of the best.

While not a psychiatrist himself, he knew that any patient who asked themselves some of those questions—and then obsessed about them afterward—was somehow questioning more than the individual parts.

Something was up with Gia and her way of thinking about Nora, her brother, and, yes, her mother too.

"Good thing," he said to himself. He nodded and

said, "good thing" once more, as he rose and walked right by Gia as he went for the closest escalator to go up to D-198 and Doctor Etter's offices. Five minutes later, he was seated in front of the doctor and they were still smiling at each other.

"Good to see you once again, Lieutenant," Doctor Etter said, and he smiled and leaned across his desk to pat Bram on the arm. "Last time was—well, you know what it was. A day that is supposed to be one of the most hallowed days for a bride and a groom, and that was... well, ruined, I guess one might say. But that was months ago, and even us medical types know that time does heal," Doctor Etter said, his voice calm and yet still on point.

Bram nodded and answered with the same measured tones. "Doctor Etter—Sam, if I might—yes, I agree with you. Last time was, well, it was a horrific experience. But that's behind us, yes," he added. Bram leaned inward a bit himself to make his pitch to the doctor. "Sam, I'm here today not on official Barony Navy business, but just for myself. I made the trip up to see you and hoped that I could convince you that the information I seek is not for me. Nor for the Navy. But for Tanner ..." he said, hoping his voice conveyed his sincerity.

Sam nodded and then tilted his head to one side. "Bram—what do you need?" he asked.

"I want to know as much as you can tell me about

227

Gia Scott—so that when I'm with Tanner, I can answer him honestly. I see it this way, Sam. That you're a doctor and have oaths and position and yadda, yadda—all of which makes your own personal opinion kept away from the rest of the world. That what you have to say, need to say, are expected to say, to the world about Gia—is maybe not so much what you think or you feel. All I want is to be able to help Tanner find a way through all of this, Sam … can you help me here?"

He knew what he asked was honest. He knew that when he was close to Lord Scott, he saw inside Tanner's psyche, and Tanner was undecided as to what to think and do about Gia. He knew not knowing what to do was a growing concern for Tanner, and Bram tried to make the doctor see that too.

Doctor Etter now leaned back and then rose to go over to the wall of bookcases beside him. Books, small knickknacks, and some plain-looking tchotchkes were all that was on his shelves, yet his hand went right to a small wooden box on one of the upper shelves. He pulled it down, sat again at his desk, and opened the box. From the box, he pulled out a fine feminine chain with a locket on it. Gold, Bram thought, or something like gold, and as Doctor Etter opened the locket with a thumbnail, he turned it so Bram could see inside.

One side held an old-fashioned photo of a young girl with very blonde hair, and the other side held what looked to be a sister with honey brown hair. Both girls were young, and both were showing big smiles and happy faces.

He pointed at the blonde girl and said, "Gia ... at, I'd think, about ten years old." Then he pointed at the facing girl and said, "And this is Nora at about eleven or twelve years old." He set the locket on the desk pad in front of him. "Gia gave this to me a few months back, for safekeeping she said. She wanted to face what she said were the lies about Nora and her brother and not 'sully' the only thing of Nora's that she owned—this picture. She said that her mother was right—that Tanner had killed Nora— and no matter what changes we'd be trying to bring to that narrative, she didn't want Nora to be a part of it," he said.

Bram said nothing and waited for the doctor to go on.

"It's a sign—at least to a psychiatrist—that there is something 'afoot' in her brain. That any talk that might occur would not affect a photo—but in fact, such talk would affect the memory. It's a good sign —and I wanted you to see that. But a caution, Bram?" he said, and his voice got steely for a bit.

"This is private between you and I. I do truly love and respect Lord Scott—and yes, I know that you are his best friend in the whole RIM Confederacy too. So I have opened up to you about this—but I will or would deny ever confirming this to anyone else ever. Gia is about twenty-five percent along in her treatment—with no real timeline either. So while I thank you for the effort to help Tanner, there is really not much new—other than this telltale," he said as he gestured to the open locket on his desk, "to offer. I will keep a close eye, of course, on all issues." He nodded to Bram as he picked up the locket and closed it. He placed it gently within the wooden box and slowly closed the lid.

As he took the escalator down to the lobby, Bram wondered what Gia was doing right now, and he smiled at the few patients around him on the way.

Doctor Etter had given him something to hope about at least; Gia was thinking for herself. He walked over to the juice bar and got in line. He smiled at those around him, and eventually he was at the front of the line.

Smiling at the youngster behind the counter, he said, "I saw someone with a juice I'd like to try. I didn't get the name of it, but it was a dark cerise in color and looked awfully thick. Would you be able to help me with that?" he asked.

The young girl behind the counter smiled back. "We only sell one of those a day to this girl—some kind of a wrestler maybe—anyways, it's Kinross Koodo fruit with double fruit—makes it a bit more expensive, though ..."

Bram nodded and placed an order for the Kinross Koodo fruit. In less than two minutes, he was walking away with the same drink he saw Gia with earlier.

He put the straw into his mouth and took a healthy pull, another, and then another. While it took a few more pulls on the straw, eventually he got some of the juice into his mouth.

Tart and acidy on the tongue. A cross between pure lemon juice and an anchovy he thought maybe, and he continued to pull on the straw to get more. He wasn't even halfway finished with the juice by the time the shuttle touched down on the Neres Navy base landing pad back on the planet.

One heck of a drink, he thought as he walked across the tarmac toward the *Atlas* and returned to his quarters.

On Neen, just before dinnertime, it was almost time for the daily recap of all the news from the RIM that usually played out with few eyes watching. Enormous screens were spread out across Neen City that were looked up at infrequently as the pedestrian traffic walked below, intent on their own lives instead of what might be news on Randi or Madrigal.

Today was different, and the crowds below had all paused to stare up at the latest news. On-screen was a vid of some type that was jumpy and shook a bit at times, as it had been an undercover vid taped. From the camera POV, a row of tanks—each holding an embryo—stretched out for what must be hundreds of yards ahead and faded in the distance. The tanks were all gray and had clear areas at the head of the tank. Each tank held small embryos, each floating in some kind of liquid. As the camera panned first to the left and then the right before turning in a full circle, it was apparent to the watchers below that this was a major medical facility. Just a few yards away, up one level from the camera, a technician in a white lab coat was making notes on his tablet, and he moved away one more tank. The lab technician was Tillion, which was easy to tell as he wore the wide-brimmed hat of that race. He made some more notes, clicked some screen buttons, and then moved on again. He held the tablet toward another new tank, and there must have been some kind of a sync as he nodded to himself, the brim of his white wide-brimmed hat flopping. He made more notes on the tablet before going to the next tank. From the camera's POV, there were more than a dozen of these white-coated technicians, all monitoring their own rows and levels of tanks.

The vid suddenly went dark, and a huge electronic board filled the screen—obviously a summary of various numbers and levels of tanks. As the image solidified on the screen, the crowd below, transfixed by the screen, gasped. Some pointed up at the numbers, and others cried out as the import of what was on-screen became apparent.

There were more than three thousand embryos in total, the sidebar read, of which thirty-nine percent were dead.

Each of those dead embryos was female.

Each, it noted, would be purged, and the tanks would be refilled at the end of the next shift cycle.

Females. Dead females only.

There was a sense within the crowd that, for some reason, Tillion did not want females, and this was their way of ensuring that only males were allowed to be born.

Everyone knew about the Tillion abhorrence of all things female. They wouldn't attend meetings with females. They wouldn't eat any kind of female food and would eat male foods only. They went out of their way to stay away from all things feminine— everyone on the RIM knew that.

And here was proof—playing in full color vid right in front of them—that Tillions killed their own females.

The crowd was upset and some chanted, "Down with the Narrisol. Down with the Narrisol ..." as they watched the vid closing out. The shock that was seen on every face increased when the voice-over and credits at the end of the video played.

"An investigation and release of the Duchy d'Avigdor," the voice-over said, the words being displayed on the screen for a full ten seconds.

More gasps echoed from the crowd of duchy citizens as they realized their government had been the creator of this video, and more angry citizens cried out about the deaths to females only.

All across Neen, from city to city and from town to town, the voices were loud and yet, at the same time, somewhat ashamed of what had been played out on screens across the planet. And played across screens all across the Duchy d'Avigdor as well.

All across the RIM Confederacy, news corps had picked up the feed, and it had played for the hundreds of billions of RIM citizens at the same time.

Somehow, the Duchy d'Avigdor had been able to get this videotape, and now it was showing it to the RIM. The citizens of the RIM were now learning what had been the Tillion secret for hundreds of years.

On Neria, in the Caliphate, the Caliph smiled to

himself as his own information began to pour in at the playing of this news vid across the RIM.

Citizens were upset—almost as much with the Duchy d'Avigdor for releasing the undercover vid as with the Tillions for their gender war. The word around the RIM was that the Duchy d'Avigdor must be made to answer for this vid and Tillion must be made to answer for its war on the female gender and the deaths of countless Tillion females.

There was no gender war, but that would only come out after the next big RIM Confederacy Council meeting. "That should be a doozy," he said to himself, his grin plastered on.

Until then, he still had almost two full weeks to work on the Duchy d'Avigdor and its Temporary Provisional Government and their ambassador to come to their aid. To help them weather this storm of protest.

He'd already heard back from the Entiran of Teuku with his own comments about what the vid had done, damage-wise, over on Tillion itself. Student uprisings. Planet-wide strikes in many industries. Their government was at a standstill. The Entiran had smiled at him from beneath the brim of a very green hat and had commented that the current Narrisol was at a loss and his name was already making the rounds with supporters when it came to replacing the current Narrisol. There had been some injuries too, he shared, at the university with those student uprisings.

All in all, the Caliph thought, just the results we were looking for …

#####

Ambassador Bedre pulled the thumb drive out of the console and sat shocked at what he'd just seen. He reached forward and picked up the clear plastic bag that held the original package that had been sent to him.

It had, he'd been told, been somehow delayed as the Provost guard who had been delivering it weeks ago had been in an accident, and the package had been gathered by the EMTs as a part of the accident and scene detritus. It had sat for that time on a shelf down at the Provost guards building until the accident investigation had been completed. Only then did someone note that the parcel was labeled as needing to go to him — and a Provost guard had delivered it just this morning. The guard who'd been injured was okay but might still lose his left leg, he'd heard, but that was not the shocking thing.

What was on the drive, the video itself, was what was shocking even though the time code stamped in the corner showed it was now ten years old.

It was a video of a medical facility on Tillion, and

it showed that Tillions were killing their female young. There was no other explanation for what he saw—and it was more than explanatory as to how Tillions treated all females here on the RIM.

Anyone who viewed this was more than likely to come to the same conclusion that he just did. Tillions killed all women—embryos really—but there was no other explanation for what he'd just seen.

He was more than aware that this kind of video, if made commonly available here on the RIM, would cause a big uproar and even more.

And yet while the vid and its contents were shocking—that was not what upset him the most. The voice-over at the end, obviously taped by someone who'd sent this to him, and the credit roll upset him the most.

"We wanted you to see what will be used to try to discredit the Barony—and this comes from the Caliph ..." the voice said as the credits rolled.

The text scrolled up from the bottom of the screen, disappearing off the top of the screen, and it read, "This is a video captured by a secret EliteGuard foray into an embryo farm on Tillion. This video is now ten years old and shows that the Barony has had knowledge of this killing of females on Tillion and has hidden it from the RIM Confederacy ... and it will be shown as an exposé coming from the Duchy d'Avigdor rather than from the Barony ..."

He flinched once again and shook his head, his white hair now plastered with sweat as he realized that this was a shock.

Whether or not it was true, the time code stamp showed that the Barony had known about this. And they'd sat on that for a decade. That spoke to him more about the Barony than Tillion.

And yet the person who'd sent him this video said that it was a ploy by the Caliph, which he fully believed.

He drummed his fingers on the desk as he thought. So ... how to ensure that the duchy would not be found at fault was the correct diplomatic question.

One, he realized in seconds, that he had an answer for at hand. He would EYES ONLY the Barony and speak directly to the Baroness.

He would offer that the Temporary Provisional Government of the Duchy d'Avigdor—him really —would find that the Barony was the winning name on the list. That the Barony and the Duchy d'Avigdor would merge under the Barony flag and that the Baroness would find herself with a realm that now encompassed sixteen planets—the largest realm in the RIM Confederacy.

The Barony then would not be able to be blamed

for this transgression, as they would be the biggest power on the RIM. The Duchy d'Avigdor would gain the shielding of that new merge with the Barony and also be found not to be at fault by all. And he would have fulfilled the mandate given to him by the duke—furthering the future of the duchy.

He didn't smile then, but he did feel like he'd done some good work on this. He dialed the Barony to request that EYES ONLY with the Baroness as he sat at the duke's desk inside his private study in the residential part of the ducal palace.

Tanner punched the pillow as quietly as he could and tried to once again get comfortable—but it just wouldn't happen. Instead, he slowly eased off the side of the bed and tried not to wake up Helena as he got up and tossed on a robe. He'd slept nude for his whole life—"Well, except for those years when I'd passed out in my uniform," he said to himself.

"Wonder how long it's been since that happened," he said, thinking back. He thought it was more than four years ago, but he couldn't be sure; time had a way of running fast in the future and slow in the past, he thought.

Don't know—but walking around his palace

bedroom fully nude was not something that a lord would do, he thought as he went over to the balcony doors and opened one quietly. He stepped out on the cool deck and silently slid the door closed behind him. Ahead, over the palace gardens and walkways, there lay the big band of the galaxy at full-blown summer shine. Summers on Neres meant that the band of the billions of galaxy stars was always overhead. Fall and winter, as the planet rotated, meant the edge of the RIM appeared, and the darkness was overwhelming at times.

But now, the starlight seemed like it was bright enough to read by, but he had nothing to read, and he dropped into a patio chair.

"AI … drone me up an iced tea," he said, and he heard the chime of the reply back to him.

Several minutes later, as he studied the big swath of stars above him, a small drone air-bot appeared coming up and over the balcony rail to land on the table before him. There was a large pitcher of iced tea and three glasses holding ice cubes and sprigs of mint—just as he liked it. He took the pitcher, poured himself a glass, and took a healthy swallow of the tea.

Cold. Tea was strong and even a bit warm before the ice took over. Mint was fresh and added a hint of flavor too.

"My future. What is it I want?" he said to himself

for the umpteenth time tonight.

That question hadn't let him get to sleep.

That question made him toss and turn.

That question had forced its way into his consciousness for the past ten months.

That question made him think back on his life and what he had accomplished so far ... and what he wanted to do with the rest of it.

"Royalty. Is that something that I really want? I am already married to the next Baroness. And if we have children, they will be Royalty too," he said, thinking out loud.

"But me? Is it for me?" he asked himself, sucking on a leaf of mint as he drained the glass.

"Being a Royal does have some advantages and I do like them. Can't evade that truth." He grinned and shook his head.

But hadn't being a plain captain of a starship been enough? That may be the whole underlying theme here, he thought as he poured himself one more glass, the pitcher now almost empty.

All I need do is to decide—the Duchy d'Avigdor or not?

No matter what he chose to do, Tanner knew it would certainly make some ripples here on the RIM. It might cause some issues with the few remaining realms on the Duchy d'Avigdor's short list too.

The Caliphate would cause him no worry at all. The Barony itself should also not be troublesome, but there was the great unknown—the Baroness—which he could not figure out how to add to the equation in order to come up with an answer. He smiled as he realized that he seemed to be more concerned with external factors than what he wanted personally.

Tanner sighed. Of course, I don't know is the answer tonight ... as it has been every night so far. Good thing I still have time to think on this. He sipped the final dregs of iced tea in his glass, stood, and stared up at the sky again.

"Stars. Billions of stars, and I'm just a small, small mote," he said to himself. "Motes matter, but until I can come up with a personal answer, not as much as one might think ..."

CHAPTER NINE

On the Barony Hospital Ship, Maddie sat with her pen poised over her notebook. Today, one of her tasks at the sanity conference meeting for Gia Scott was to record notes for the meeting. "Then there's no doubt, Doctor Trystan, is there? After almost eleven months of group sessions, your most updated diagnosis of the patient is that she is sane. And, as a result of those sessions, she now is what a layman would call better?" Doctor Etter asked.

Doctor Trystan, the head psychiatrist whose area of specialization was group sessions, nodded. As he combed his hair back with a hand, the white locks fell back to hover above his ear. "That's true, Doctor Etter. After almost eleven months—well, you know how it is. Most patients sit in the group but outside the general exploration of their own troubles for a month or so. Gia did that too, but she joined in as soon as the topic of justice came up one day. She ranted—quite well, I'd add—that justice must always be the goal—no matter if it was done by the government or citizens. Since those days, however, she has realized that vigilantism is something that is not an acceptable part of being a citizen, and that is a good thing, we all know. Add in that about five months ago, when the group delved deeply into parental love and authority, she made some great strides in beginning to understand about her own mother. And the belief in the guilt of her brother, being the major factor that she admitted only two weeks ago, had been faulty. Stored in her psyche by a parent, and in fact, as she said just yesterday, not true."

Doctor Trystan leaned back in his chair and sighed. "Getting that kind of a new thought, from any patient, is a wonderful thing to a psychiatrist. Yes, we worked hard at showing her the ways to think about Lord Scott, and yes, she went down the typical hatred paths—but now, I do fully believe that she is no longer blaming Tanner for her sister's death. She was Tanner's sister too, she said out loud just a few days ago like it was a revelation to her— though it's been true forever," he added.

He looked over at Maddie and smiled. "She had some help too, I understand, from our best nurse practitioner—Maddie Nelson—who dutifully reported back on her state of mind and all of those unanswered questions too. Thank you, Maddie," he said.

Seated across the table from him, Maddie smiled and blushed.

Doctor Etter smiled too. "Doctor Nelson, anything to add, GP-wise?" he asked.

Doctor Nelson, the general practitioner, smiled and didn't open a folder or his tablet. "Not a thing. She's as healthy as a horse, and I might add that those horrible scars on her back and lower rear thighs are all perfectly healed—older scar tissue too. We did offer to remove them with cosmetic surgery, but she rebuffed any of that. Said that she needed those reminders of days gone by. No amount of questions or pleadings by me would get her to spell out how she'd been hurt that way," he said as he looked around the room.

Everyone else shook their heads as well.

"It's as I thought—an event that I think may well never come to light. But, she seems to not be bothered by same. Physically, she's as lithe and flexible and strong as any athlete I've ever treated. She's a clerk on leave from Gallipedia—which in and of itself is a whole new issue. But she is healthy beyond her peers, and by quite a margin."

Doctor Etter nodded and glanced over at

Maddie. "Let the record show that she is healthy—I think maybe we'll leave off the clerk part, agreed?"

All the heads in the room nodded, and Maddie said, "Acknowledged, Doctor," and she made notes to the meeting minutes.

Doctor Etter then looked down at his folder and picked up a paper. "Then, if we all agree, we will notify the courts that one Gia Scott, after almost eleven months of treatment and study, has been judged sane. Since she has been determined to be compos mentis, as the courts term it, we will need to notify them later today, Maddie—normal channels, please."

Maddie leaned forward now. "Doctor—do I also send notice to her legal counsel too? That attorney Jordan Alpert has been messaging me every single week, awaiting the sanity conference results—do I tell him too?" she asked.

Doctor Etter nodded. "Yes, both the courts, which will handle the prosecution of the patient, and her defense counsel should receive the same notification at the same time," he answered.

"We all realize, that now being found sane, this means that she will face a trial for those two murders," Maddie stated.

Again, all the heads in the room nodded.

Doctor Nelson, addressed that point. "Yes, but our report will include that in our opinion—a medical opinion—that she was delusional up until recently. Because brainwashing is such an invasive form of influence, it requires the complete isolation and dependency of the subject, which is why you mostly hear of brainwashing occurring in prison camps or totalistic cults," he said.

Doctor Etter followed up on that point too. "The agent—Gia's mother—had complete control over the target—in this case, Gia—so that sleep patterns, eating, using the bathroom, and the fulfillment of other basic human needs depended on the will of the agent. In the brainwashing process, the agent systematically breaks down the target's identity to the point that it doesn't work anymore. The agent then replaces it with another set of behaviors, attitudes, and beliefs that work in the target's current environment. It was this way that Gia's mother used her position of being the only parent to inflict on her surviving daughter the belief that Tanner had killed Nora ..."

"And," Doctor Trystan added, "it was that delusional indoctrination that we eventually were able to get Gia to see was untrue just recently. She is sane. And, yes, there will be consequences for her crimes but all mitigated by her delusional state at the time. I'd think that she may well get a year or two—suspended, of course, as others we've been involved with have been found guilty before," he added.

That too got nods.

With the full medical diagnosis of Gia's delusional behavior, not one of them thought Gia would receive much of a sentence when she was found guilty.

#####

She threw the whole glass, wine and all, over her shoulder, and the smash on the fancy marble floor was loud.

"Piss off, AI," she spat.

The robo-vacs that had jumped out of the wall sconces returned to their location in seconds. The Baroness was mad, and the simple housekeeping AI had responded as quickly as they could.

"Seal the room, Baroness code W-3," she barked.

The palace-wide AI made a note, and the doors to the room were locked and sealed. No one would be allowed to enter—as long as her body vitals read within acceptable standards.

She rose, trooped over to the console, and said, "Replay at seventy-five percent speed."

There was an almost imperceptible hesitation, and then the screen darkened once more. She watched the entire vid for the third time.

She watched the white-coated medical lab tech as he went from embryo tank to embryo tank, making notes on his tablet, it seemed.

She watched as some of the tanks in the rows that lay ahead seemed to have an alert light flashing. Nothing indicated what the emergency might be.

With the sidebar display included in the video, it was apparent to her, and she was sure to billions here on the RIM, that these were tanks growing Tillion males. Only males. No live females as the sidebar noted there were hundreds of tanks with deceased embryos—all female. Tillions were selectively killing their female gender embryos.

She couldn't care less. But she, like the other billions who were watching this vid, could see that this vid wore the telltale icon of a Barony EliteGuard vid editing suite, via the time-stamp that dated this video ten years back.

She had never seen this, but she would get to the bottom of this vid and its camera crew soon, she knew.

The closing credits were what really angered her though. The closing credits read, "This is a video captured by a secret EliteGuard foray into an embryo farm on Tillion. This video is now ten years old and shows that the Barony has had knowledge of this killing of females on Tillion and has hidden it from the RIM Confederacy ..."

Never mind the Tillions. Why had someone labeled this as a Barony-run project? Her foot tapped harder on the floor. Why ... and more importantly, who ...

The Baroness sighed. Now she somehow had to arrange to get back into the good graces of the Duchy d'Avigdor as the short-list favorite.

#####

Tanner marched as only a Royal—a Barony Royal—could through the palace doors and inside the public access point that he'd walked into time and time again. As a Royal, he had no EliteGuard to act as his guide—though truthfully, behind him about twenty paces, he was followed by his own security detail.

He was anxious about this meeting with the Baroness, as the topic today was Gia. He had no idea as to what the medical team had found up on the Barony Hospital Ship, but a private message from Maddie had said only good luck. Probably couldn't send more than that and not run afoul of the Barony security forces, he thought.

He went around the massive table made from one section of a tree trunk that must have been at least thirty feet across. This time, the enormous vase, which had been on that table for years, was floating above the table by a foot or two. He slowed to take a better look. As he dipped his head to peer under the vase as best as he could, he realized that the bottom of the vase was on a copper plate.

He grinned. "Looks like the Baroness likes to use the newfound anti-grav for even palace decor," he said to himself.

After three more minutes of walking, he eventually found himself at the only open door in the great stateroom, and he entered the parlor off its right side.

In the room, he made his way over to the side table and helped himself to an iced tea. There was even fresh mint, which he usually had to request.

He sat on a loveseat and took a swig from his glass, as the Baroness entered from behind a wall hanging off to his left.

He was surprised, but his wife entered the room right behind her, and she half-smiled at him as she came over to sit beside him.

The Baroness was in all shades of what he'd have called yellow. Better not mention her yellow outfit. Most likely, I'll hear that her blouse is chartreuse and the leggings are avocado and spring bud, he thought and snickered internally. Anyways, more important points for me to ponder.

Helena was already there and had come in with the Baroness. He'd not been told, which was highly unusual. Hmm … makes a man—a husband— wonder.

"Lord Scott—the medical reports are in from our

Hospital Ship," the Baroness said, her voice soft.

He nodded.

"And she has been found sane. Compos mentis, they say in the courts. So, it's time for her to stand trial for her crimes, Tanner," she said even more quietly.

He looked at Helena, but there was no hint of anything there for him. He looked back at the Baroness. "Ma'am—was there not also a full diagnosis of what state her mind was in at the time of the ... the time of ... at the wedding," he said, his voice catching only twice.

The Baroness waved it off. "Yes, but not worth even thinking on—the doctors said she was delusional, but that does not help at all. She will stand trial, and she will be found guilty. No one can doubt that—least of all you," she said, her voice now strong and almost strident.

"But Ma'am—those are mitigating circumstances, they're called. I know. I checked and her attorney will use them to try to get her the lightest sentence possible. Something that I'm in favor of, Ma'am." There. He'd said it. He had waffled on this now for months, but the die had been cast.

The Baroness pulled back somewhat in surprise, he thought, before she answered him. "It matters not what the defense will argue. I am the Baroness, and the courts will decide as I see fit. And I am sorry to say but to deliver the Barony from all further loss of reputation, we will need to find her guilty—she is guilty, Lord Scott, just look down at your own chest if you doubt me. Once found guilty, there is no other sentence for murder—two murders, in fact, both capital offenses—than death. It's what lies ahead for her.

"And I might add that we will make both the Issians on Eons and the Duchy d'Avigdor as happy as can be for taking on the role of executioner of the assassin who killed their own heads of state. While they have some standing here, they've left it to us …" she finished off.

He was numb. There had never been any talk of death for Gia. There had never been any talk of any kind of a sentence either. It was supposed to be up to him to decide this—Gia was his sister, after all.

Yet now, it had been decided. Gia was to die.

And beside him, her nails on one hand clenched into his thigh, his wife sat quietly. She wanted him to say nothing, which he understood from her vice-like grip on his thigh.

He wanted to stand and tell the Baroness that this would not happen her way. Why she'd chosen to ensure that Gia was to die was beyond him. He grimaced back at her, as he realized it was beyond his level of Royalty to make any different type of choice.

He nodded to the Baroness and sipped from his iced tea once more, shredding the whole sprig of mint in seconds. He knew there was one card that could yet be played … one that might change much in the RIM Confederacy.

He sat at the table on the balcony again. Instead of iced tea, the drink in front of him was a glass of the best Quaran chardonnay there is—or was, as the glass was now empty.

He still felt that he was immune to any kind of effects of alcohol, but he enjoyed the taste of the wine. It was oaky and had hints of a sort of buttery flavor—yet it had a toffee flavor to it too that he loved.

But he would feel none of the positives or negatives from drinking alcohol. He could drink wine with anyone and be as cold sober after many, many bottles as he was before he had one sip, but as usual, the person across from him was not sober.

Helena sat just staring at him with no glass in front of her. She had taken a sip out of his glass twice, but that was all. If she had drank as many glasses as Tanner had, she would be having a hard time staying upright in her seat about now.

He looked up at the full swing of the galaxy of stars overhead and then back down at her. "Yes, let's do it," he said in answer to the question that she had asked more than ten minutes ago.

He had played with the question. He had looked at it now for almost eleven months, with no answer. He had had countless sleepless nights and felt awful the next day from the lack of sleep. He had avoided the question now for almost a year. And today, he had decided what he wanted to do.

Helena had opened up the conversation just an hour ago after the meeting with the Baroness had ended and they'd returned to their own area of the palace..

Death. Gia was to die. Not on my watch, he thought. Gia is my last living relative—and I owe it to Nora to try to save her at least.

Helena had spoken about what might happen to them both. She had, he'd suddenly realized, decided that he, her husband, was worth more than the inheritance of the Barony—at least in public. Privately, she had said her blood would guarantee that when the current Baroness died, she would inherit same.

Or so she believed, she had admitted with a shrug. Until then, she would be his wife—the Duchess of d'Avigdor by title.

He smiled at her and kissed her fully on the lips. She kissed him back but squirmed away from his grasp and grinned at him. "Well, Duke, please, let's get the planning working, shall we, before we celebrate?"

He shook his head at her. "Figures, being a duke is going to be about as much fun as being a lord is—was, perhaps better put" he said.

She nodded and clicked the tablet in front of her to make some notes. "Right," she said, "first, we'll need a constitutional expert—that Professor Boven, right?"

He nodded and the planning went on for more than an hour.

"And lastly, the Agenda. Do we notify Chairman Gramsci via the RIM Confederacy Council clerk that we want to be on the Agenda?" she asked.

"No, let's leave that for me—I'll arrange it via Admiral McQueen," he said and smiled.

Time to call in a chit or two ... he thought.

She was surprised by the EYES ONLY from Lord Scott, but then she smiled to herself.

Knowing what someone right in front of you was thinking was one thing. When that person was light years away, it took more than innate talent. It took experience, and she knew that it would come one day.

She nodded to her aide, whose name she had forgotten. She focused and the name Adele filled her mind, and she smiled. This is easy across a room, but when light years away from the person? One day, it will be just as easy for me, she thought.

She waited, and on the close wall, the screen suddenly went full white and then dissolved into the Barony icon of the twin crowns on the red and blue shield. Moments later, Lord Scott appeared, and sitting beside him was his wife Helena, the Lady St. August.

The Master Adept bowed her head and then smiled as she began to speak. "Lord Scott and Lady St. August, what a nice surprise," she said.

They smiled back and both spoke at once. "Master Adept—" Then they looked at each other, and the Lady smiled and dipped her chin to her husband for him to continue.

"Master, we come to you with a proposition—in fact, one that we see as a true win-win for both Eons and the Duchy d'Avigdor," he began.

Odd, she thought, that he didn't mention the Barony but instead the duchy ... more to this than meets the eye.

"Ma'am," he said, "this is about the future of my sister—Gia Scott, the woman who we all know shot and killed both your own predecessor, the then Master Adept, and the Duke d'Avigdor. She has been judged to be sane by the Barony Hospital Ship and returned to Neres City to the courts. There will

be a trial; at which time, she will be found guilty
and sentenced to death," he said, his voice almost
bleak.

The Master Adept nodded. She had expected
this, and that it was news to Lord Scott was a bit
surprising. She let that sit for a moment and then
asked softly, "And why would this be of interest to
Eons—and to me?"

"Ma'am, I am not going to allow that to happen. I
intend to stop that, by forcing the Barony to turn
over my sister to me, and I will take charge of her
future—not her death," he said.

The Master Adept sat back on her couch and
smiled at the man in front of her on the screen.

"But that might be a tough thing to accomplish,
for a lord—seeing as the Barony is led by a full
Baroness, who we were told welcomes the death
penalty for the assassin. We were asked if we would
allow the Barony to handle the prosecution of the
prisoner, and we agreed to that, as did, we
understand, the Duchy d'Avigdor—well, their
provisional leader, the Ambassador, did as well,"
he said and nodded.

She noted that Helena grabbed him by the arm,
slowing him down perhaps—she couldn't tell. And
then her mind leapt for the answer, and she knew
what he was about to say.

He looked away for a second and then back at

her. "I am the Option Number Two, Ma'am, for the Duchy d'Avigdor and their future. I am going to accept the duke's gift and take the title of the new Duke d'Avigdor—and I am asking that when I do, that you—on behalf of all Issians and Eons—follow my lead when, on behalf of the duchy, I ask for the Barony to turn over the prisoner for us to handle her prosecution. It is a point of law that as no Barony citizen was injured by the crime, that they will need to turn over the prisoner to the aggrieved parties—the duchy in this case, Ma'am," he said.

He'd had legal help with that conundrum, she realized, and he was right, she thought. She was floored but knew that under these new circumstances, she would be more than glad to help the new duke attain the future of his sister. By doing so, she would forever have a favor she could call upon from the man.

And as she nodded and said pleasantries during their goodbyes, she couldn't help but think *what this might mean to the RIM Confederacy—and what a new power like Duke Scott might bring to the RIM too.*

CHAPTER TEN

The admiral entered the RIM Confederacy
Council chamber and noted that his pre-meeting
changes to the room had been received and acted
upon. Outside in the long hallway, he'd just walked
by eight Juno Provost guards, stationed along the
hall, who were armed and standing on picket duty.
If asked, they were to simply say that it was a local
Juno holiday, which it was some kind of a
commemorative ex-ruler's birthday, he thought,
and he was grateful for that. At the doorway to the
actual chamber stood two more Provost guards. He
knew these two personally, and he had chosen them
after much deliberation. They were loyal and able
to follow orders no matter what the orders were.
He was glad such men still existed in the guard—
and yet a part of him wondered at the much

younger group of guards who'd ask questions
before pulling the trigger on order. He shrugged.
Not his business today.

Inside the chamber, it was as it always was, still
getting some minor attention from the chef de
mission on the table arrangements, measuring for
those "must be exactly equal" dimensions for things
like desk pads and water glasses.

As usual, McQueen ignored same, went to his
spot behind the empty chairman's seat, and
dropped his meeting items, folders, and tablet
down on his desk up one tier from the chamber
floor. He turned then to look around and wondered
if this was what he'd still be seeing in a couple of
hours—a room with no appearance of any
aftermath of what would be one of the most
uproarious meetings ever on the RIM.

Off to his left on the enormous horseshoe-shaped
table, a couple techies were making small updates
and changes to the water seats the DenKoss
members would be using. The perches for the
Djarreer members were still missing, and as he
looked at the doorway, the perches for their use
came in on a dolly, handled by more techies.
Against the far wall, a tiny telltale red point of light
above the doorway to one of the alcoves showed
him the chamber AI was up and running fine. He'd
made the requests as only the admiral of the RIM

Confederacy Navy could, and he had gotten some extra security thresholds input into the room's AI. While they were probably never going to be used, it was still a possibility that some members might become angry during the upcoming meeting, and he wanted to be ready for that too.

He looked over to his right and noted that the chair the ambassador would be seated in, representing the Duchy d'Avigdor, was as properly positioned as all the rest of the realms around the table.

He grunted and said to himself, "Fine for now." "But for the meeting to come, maybe not so fine."

He went out to the hallway to await his guests. He'd asked them to come early, and they were arriving now. He smiled and made introductions. He led his three guests into the chamber and nodded as they all commented about how big and beautiful the room was with its massive table and the raised tiers that ran around the outside of same. The chief justice of the Duchy Supreme Court shared that she had been here once before, as a part of a school trip, but she had no real memory of the size and solemn nature of the room.

As they walked around the table, the constitutional expert, Professor Bowen from Carnarvon University in Veloka said, "As always, rooms like this need to be big, spacious, and above all, highly held in regard by the citizenry that it served."

"Dunno if served might be the verb to use in this case," Admiral Higgins, the third of McQueen's guests, said, as they walked up and mounted the few steps to take their seats as guests behind Admiral McQueen's seat.

As the fleet admiral for the Barony Navy, Admiral Higgins was seated in the guest area behind the seat—or close to the area where the Baroness would sit later—so he was not far away from where he should be seated.

Admiral McQueen spoke to the three of them about the upcoming meeting and the Agenda as well as what to expect. He was more than honest, and the only reaction to his little speech was the chief justice letting out a small gasp.

Each of his three guests had agreed to be there to perform their duties, and all had sworn to him that they'd kept their upcoming presence at the meeting a hidden part of their schedules back at home. And all had kept their word as well as successfully kept their plans secret, as the RIM Navy intel had been unable to find any kind of waffling by any of the three of them or even a hint of a whisper that either of the three would be in Juno on this day.

He nodded to them and smiled. "Remember, we're here today—the four of us—to make sure the

RIM Confederacy Constitution is followed to the letter of the law. History will record what happens here at a later date—but today, we just do our jobs."

All three heads in front of him nodded, and he nodded back to them.

In the next half hour, RIM Confederacy members rolled in, and other than the normal slopping of some water onto the floor over in the DenKoss seating area, all was as it should have been. McQueen leaned on his desk. He nodded and said his hellos to various members as they arrived, and he smiled at the Duchy d'Avigdor ambassador who came over directly to where he was standing.

"May I ask, Chief Justice, why you're here today and why I wasn't told you'd be coming? Perhaps we could have shared a ship ..." Ambassador Bedre said as he stood before the tier of seats.

"Yes, Ambassador, I took the Council up on their standing offer to attend a Council meeting in person—and I thought it apropos that it be one with our own ambassador sitting in the Duchy d'Avigdor realm seat," she said back nicely.

The ambassador didn't blush, but her polite compliment still reached him, and he nodded and made small talk to her for a full minute more before going back to his seat at the big table.

McQueen thought that had gone well, and just as he had that thought, the Baroness strode into the

Council chamber, making her way to her chair just in front of him, and she stopped when she saw her Barony Navy fleet admiral.

"Admiral Higgins, how nice to have you here. May I inquire as to what the occasion is? Surely the Juno holiday is not enough to warrant any kind of notice to a navy man," she said.

He smiled at her. "No, Ma'am, just visiting with Admiral McQueen, and we're going to be working on navy matters across the RIM later today—so I thought I'd take in a Council meeting too," he said.

As she nodded and left them to take her seat, McQueen thought the admiral hadn't been totally incorrect, and he smiled at him as he took his seat as the Council clerk rose.

Across the room, the Provost guards closed the door as the Council meeting was about to start.

The chairman nodded to the clerk and banged the gavel down on the desk. Conversation dried up as he said, "This meeting of the RIM Confederacy Council will come to order, please. Clerk, the Agenda, please ..."

The clerk read off the meeting Agenda, referring to the printed page in front of her, as she stood at the clerk's console in the center of the big horseshoe-shaped table. "This meeting will come to order, and our Agenda is as follows. Regrets first from Garnuth and Novertag. Garnuth, it appears, is facing a major outbreak of porcine fever, we've been told, and Novertag is in the middle of their election week. Both have offered to receive full minutes and to allow the chairman to vote their own views by proxy. Any challenges to that offer?" she asked.

The room was silent with no rejections of same, and the clerk nodded to the chairman.

"Carried," he said and then nodded back.

"Next, our Agenda, you see in front of you, has been slightly modified, and my apologies on that note. I only received notice of the addition of this item minutes ago—"

The member from Carnarvon interrupted her. "Clerk, not a problem—let's just move on, shall we? I'm sure whomever or whatever it's about will be obvious to us all," he said.

Most members agreed with him and either nodded or knocked on the tabletop.

Point taken, McQueen thought.

Chairman Gramsci looked around the table and said, "Then the modified Agenda is accepted by all —and carried."

The clerk motioned to her staffers, and shortly thereafter, the clerk's two staffers quickly circled the table and handed out the modified Agenda, which had just been printed.

All eyes looked down at the sheet of paper, and

then all eyes looked up and over to the admiral who was standing up at his tiered seat.

"My compliments to the clerk and the chairman for the opportunity to speak first at today's Council meeting. I am going to, perhaps, be held accountable for what is about to happen here—but there is someone that I'd like to introduce to the Council first. Council AI, please open the outer doors to admit my guest," he said, and as he did, the doors opened, and all eyes turned away from the admiral toward the door.

Standing in the hallway, facing the now opened double doors, was Lord Scott, wearing the pure white uniform of a Duchy d'Avigdor Navy officer, with no rank visible at all. As he entered the room, several seated members called out.

"There is no reason that this Royal need to attend the meeting—his Baroness is already here," one said.

"What kind of outfit is that?" another said.

"Admiral, surely there are real items to deal with rather than another Barony issue," a third said.

McQueen had no idea if that referred to the recent vid that had come out or not, and he was about to reply when Tanner spoke up, steel in his voice.

"Members of the RIM Confederacy Council, I come before you today to claim my place among you," he said.

That quieted the room for a moment, and then protests that a Barony lord could not sit with them rang out through the chamber, followed by others stating that this Council was composed of heads of state only—and he was not that. "Was not the Baroness the one that ruled the Barony?" someone yelled.

Tanner nodded to the yells and even to a catcall or two, and then he walked over to stand close to Ambassador Bedre, sitting in the Duchy d'Avigdor's seat at the table.

"Ambassador Bedre, I charge you with the duty to report to the Council truthfully—as you presented here to the Council months ago—that there is a second option, is there not, in the duke's will—a codicil, I believe it's called?"

The ambassador blanched but nodded his agreement.

The Caliph rose in anger, his voice loud in the chamber, standing up to his full height of six feet and six inches. "This is all not to be allowed," he said, pointing a finger at the admiral, "as we have already heard that there has been a decision on the successful new realm to be formed with the Duchy d'Avigdor becoming a part of the Caliphate." His voice grew louder and louder until he was yelling.

Before Admiral McQueen could even react,

Provost guards were double-timing it into the chamber to take up posts around the room. Each was armed with a Merkel—an automatic rifle that could project ten rounds a second. Not a single head of state in the room missed that as they stared and looked first at each other and then at Admiral McQueen.

McQueen nodded to them and then spoke to the Chairman, with respect. "Chairman Gramsci, my apologies at this, um, this intrusion of the Provost guards, but I thought it might be a very contentious meeting—well, at least my own number one presentation, so I had them come in and take up posts within the room to prevent any kind of violence. They do not respond to me, Chairman, but only to you, is that not correct, Captain Ankers?" he said to the guard in charge of the detail.

"Sir, yes, Sir. We've been instructed to follow only the chairman's orders from now on, Sir," he said, barking out the answer.

Voices rose once again in the chamber room, and all clamored for recognition by the chairman, but the four gavels Chairman Gramsci banged on the desk eventually got the room back in some degree of order.

"Noted, Admiral McQueen—and yes, I am in charge. This is highly unusual, but I think perhaps warranted—but next time, Admiral, give me some advance notice, please," he said as four of his hands dropped the gavels on the tabletop. He nodded to Lord Scott to continue as he motioned for the Caliph to be seated.

"As you were about to say, and out loud, please, Ambassador, for the record—about Option Number Two in the late duke's will?" Tanner said.

"Yes, Lord Scott—there is a codicil, whereby the duke left the inheritance of the duchy—the dukedom itself—to a secret person here on the RIM. But, might I point out that there has already been a final choice for our Option Number One made in the Duchy d'Avigdor and its future—"

"You may certainly do that—but as that is point number four in today's Agenda, and we're only on point number one—carried by the Council just moments ago, we will not hear that yet.

"Instead, please tell the Council who the duke chose to inherit the duchy—should they wish to do so—in one year from his death. One year, by the way, that is not over for thirteen days," Tanner said.

McQueen had insisted that he add that to his explanation. He had told Tanner there was no sense in allowing any misunderstanding for today's events. The room got deadly silent again as the Council members waited to hear Ambassador Bedre reveal the duke's heir. McQueen noted that the Provost guards were ready for anything.

Ambassador Bedre squirmed in his chair. His face was white and all present could see sweat on his brow. He wiped his brow with a handkerchief and grimaced. "The duke—David—determined that the person he wanted to inherit the duchy was you, Lord Scott," he said.

Again, the room exploded. The Djarreer member actually took to wing and squawked. The DenKoss members swished in their tanks, and water poured over the sides. Leudie neck snakes suddenly uncoiled, and some snapped at the air. The Eran giant almost rose up to his full twelve feet, then remembered the ceiling was only inches away, and sank back down.

All were surprised, McQueen noted, except for the Master Adept who looked around the room at face after face, reading, he thought, what lay behind these displays of surprise. She knew. And that was something he'd have to file away for later consideration.

Tanner nodded. "Then here, by the strength of the duke's codicil, I hereby accept the position of the new Duke d'Avigdor. Chief Justice, if you please," he said.

The room was silent once again as they all turned to look up in the tiered guest seating behind the chairman.

The chief justice accepted the hand of Admiral Higgins as they both descended from the guest area to approach Tanner, and she stopped just short of him. She smiled at him, and with Admiral Higgins' help, she placed a bible in the admiral's hands and asked Tanner to place his left hand on same.

He did so and held up his right hand, palm open and facing the woman.

"Please repeat after me. I —say your name—, hereby swear that I will faithfully execute the position of the Duke d'Avigdor and will, to the best of my ability, preserve, protect, and defend the constitution of the duchy—so help me God."

Tanner did just that, and in moments, there were even a few cheers from around the table.

"Ambassador," Tanner said nicely, "please give me my seat."

The ambassador half-smiled up at his new duke, rose, and offered Tanner the seat at the Council table reserved for the head of state for the Duchy d'Avigdor.

More cheers and even a few shouts of "Attaboy" greeted his new role on the RIM.

The Baroness, however, did not cheer at all; instead, she rose in her seat.

Bingo, McQueen thought, now this gets interesting.

"May I ask Ambassador Bedre then—as the

notice of the awarding of the duchy to the successful suitor for same is still upcoming on the Agenda—if this will still occur?"

Before the ambassador could answer, Chairman Gramsci pounded his gavel on the table and said, "Baroness—the new head of state for the duchy—Duke Scott—might be the one to ask that question to, I'd think?"

That got knocks on the table in agreement.

The Baroness smiled at Tanner. "And the answer then to my question would be?" she posed sweetly.

As sweet as a hungry Jael, McQueen thought.

"Baroness, I am glad to answer your query. There is a new head of state for the Duchy d'Avigdor and we, as of now, no longer need to think about merging with any other realm. So item number four is hereby removed from the rest of the Agenda. Clerk to make a note of that now, please," he said, which got a nod from the clerk who was busy recording all of this, her face as white as others in the room.

"I am sorry to hear of that, as the Barony was to be the new realm of the Duchy d'Avigdor," she said, which got more stunned looks around the table. But no one said a word, as what might have been mattered not a whit.

The Caliph slammed the table in front of him, and more than a few safeties on the Provost's

Merkels could be heard snapping to off.

But he sat still.

McQueen almost thought that was too bad; the erasure of such a head of state might have been a good thing overall for the RIM Confederacy, but he pushed that thought away.

"However, Baroness—we do have some other business to present with the chairman's approval on this minor addition to our spot on the Agenda," Tanner said, and he got a nod from the chairman on that, so he went ahead.

"There will be a major change to the Duchy d'Avigdor's position on the Barony holding the prisoner charged with the murder of both the previous Master Adept and the previous Duke d'Avigdor. We understand that the duchy had been asked—as one of the realms that was affected by the crime—to allow the Barony to look after the prosecution of the charged criminal.

"We hereby rescind that permission and request that the prisoner be readied for transport over to Neen by end of business today. We will look after the prosecution of that prisoner on our own," he said calmly.

Quiet. The room was quiet, and McQueen knew a large part of the day rested on how the Baroness would respond. He was thankful for the Provost guards and the overall eye of the chamber AI as well.

"Do I take it that the people of Eons do likewise," she asked, looking over at the Master Adept at the table.

The Master smiled at her. "Yes, please, Baroness. As one of the two realms that were affected by this crime, we ask that the prisoner be turned over to the Duchy d'Avigdor for prosecution," she said, her voice as serene as waves on a nighttime sea.

The Baroness just stared at her for a second, and then nodded. "I will make it so, Duke Scott," she said and dipped her head.

Bloodshed averted, McQueen thought, or at least a fat lip or two.

"And there is one more matter, Baroness—but I turn over that nicety to Admiral Higgins, the Barony fleet admiral."

Higgins walked over to stand beside the Baroness and half-smiled at her. "I am afraid that I must tender my resignation, Baroness. Also, the resignation of Lieutenant Commander Bram Sander from the Barony Navy. It's been a slice, but other opportunities call, Ma'am," he said as he set two large envelopes with the proper paperwork enclosed in front of her.

She sighed and then nodded.

And in one stroke, the Duchy d'Avigdor's Navy had a brand new admiral and lieutenant commander loyal to the new duke, McQueen thought, and that brought a grin to his face, which spread around the table to the faces of other members once they caught on.

But, McQueen thought, something was odd about the Baroness and her acceptance of losing a realm and two of her best officers too. There was the larger matter of how uncomfortable the next holiday dinner might be at the Barony Palace when Duke Scott and his wife came to sup, but that was for someone else to worry about. Still something else left unsaid and unnoticed, but what? Admiral McQueen sighed. He would have to wait to see how that unknown would present itself in the future.

The room was quiet so McQueen spoke. "Clerk, I believe that this ends my own presentation as Agenda item number one ..." he said nicely.

She nodded and looked at Chairman Gramsci.

"Agreed, Admiral McQueen. Let me be one of the first to acknowledge our newest head of state on the RIM Confederacy Council—Duke Tanner Scott of the Duchy d'Avigdor. Welcome, Sir," he said, and all over the chamber, there were congratulatory shouts and knocking on the table that lasted a full two minutes.

The chairman let it go and then had to use two gavels at once to ask the room for quiet so the meeting could resume. "Clerk, please ensure to record all of these items carefully for the record and for the minutes that will need to be sent out as well. Item number one carried. Item number two, please ..." he said, and the meeting continued.

#####

Helena had not been able to get into the Council meeting, but she and Lieutenant Commander Sander had watched over the closed loop vid in the room next door that was reserved for VIP viewing.

When her husband walked out of the Council chamber, she grabbed him and gave him a huge hug. "I am so proud of the new Duke d'Avigdor—you are my hero," she said, and he grinned back at her as he held her tight.

"You are mine," he said and kissed her at length.

Bram shook his hand more than long enough, and the two friends grinned at each other.

From her pocket, Helena took out a small box and opened it, giving it to Bram to hold for her. From within the box, she took out the Duchy d'Avigdor icon—three red planets around a blue sun—and she worried them into place on Tanner's collar. "There," she said as she stepped back—"the new Duke d'Avigdor in all his glory."

Tanner smiled and accepted their congratulations as the whole group smiled and clapped for him.

They accompanied their small group of two admirals and the chief justice down to the ground level of Navy Hall and made their goodbyes.

Tanner clasped McQueen's hand extra hard and shook it with vigor. "Won't forget—could never forget—what you've done for me once again, Admiral," he said, true friendship in his voice.

McQueen had shuffled his feet and smiled back at his protege. "Never been close to a duke before," he said. "Just remember I like Scotch," he said as a throwaway line, and they both grinned at that.

The chief justice was joining Admiral Higgins for the ride back to Neres City in the Barony.

"Will be in touch, Admiral," Tanner said, and they too gripped hands like true friends.

After the congratulations and goodbyes had finished, Bram, Tanner, and Helena returned to the *Sword*.

Bram sat in the co-pilot's seat, and every once in a while, he shouted back at Tanner and Helena that he'd never been so close to Royalty. That got a laugh from them all.

"We need to make some plans," Tanner said.

Helena nodded, turned on her PDA, and hit the holo-switch. What popped up was a list Tanner should have known that she'd have made, and she went through each item one by one.

"The prisoner will be picked up at the Hospital

Ship—I insisted on this too, by the way—at seventeen hundred hours by the Duchy d'Avigdor Navy's cruiser, the DN GoldEye. She will be moved into the palace—in the palace brig, mind you—by nineteen hundred hours and looked at by our own med team. We will get that report later—with full med screen scans too. We good on that one?" she asked.

He nodded. Couldn't have done it better myself. Checking her meds was a good one too …

"The *Sword*—this ship itself. I know how much you love this one, so I've begun negotiations between our navy purchasing department and the Barony. No idea on what the price might be—but we'll get word back soonest. Okay?"

He nodded once more, thinking he was a lucky duke for sure.

"Third, today, is the duchy itself. We'll need to make an announcement to the citizens of same—so I've arranged for a full spectrum of press and media and even RIM Confederacy-wide news teams to meet with us at the ducal palace this evening at twenty hundred hours. Full media scrum, so you better have that smile ready—and a side note? You are the first duke in centuries that does not carry the d'Avigdor bloodline. Some will make you answer for that, and I'd go with the fact that David thought you so capable he named you as his heir. Professor

279

Bowen," she said as she looked up a couple of rows at their constitutional expert, "will be with us for a short—I told him less than four minutes— explanation about the legality of the inheritance on same."

Professor Bowen sat alone, looking out the starboard porthole on that side of the *Sword*, and did not respond to Helena saying his name.

Tanner nodded once more. "Maybe I could just go back to Bottle and lie on the beach and Helena could run the duchy," he mumbled.

The words were no sooner out of his mouth than she held up a finger to wag in his face. "Fat chance. You were probably in 'duke land' and missed point number seven today at the Council meeting, but Bottle has now joined the Barony, who now has eleven planets. Twelve when Ghayth votes in about a year or so. So while the Baroness missed out on the Duchy d'Avigdor today, she still increased her realm by a planet. Talk about ego," she said.

Tanner could tell that Helena was as impressed as he was, as Bottle had seemed to be of the mindset that existence as an independent was what they were all about. Yet, somehow, they had just joined the Barony. Something was up with that too, he knew, and he wondered how that was going to play out.

"Final thought—and I see you're in that space

too. As a duke, you need to think on bigger issues—
Confederacy-wide issues. Spaceships and the like,
you leave to those who serve you. Your job will be
to govern ... something that I know only some of—
but will, of course, help all I can."

Tanner stopped her. "Helena, might it be
possible to get my aide—Lieutenant Ayla Kiraz—
away from the Barony Navy too? Or, is that too
much to ask what with all the happenings of
today?" he wondered.

Within seconds, Helena was busy making notes
on her PDA, and a moment later, she patted his
arm. "I will check first on whether or not she might
like to come over to the Duchy d'Avigdor Navy—
course, it'll all be one navy one day when I take
over the Barony," she said with a wicked grin on
her face. She dropped her hand onto his arm, and
he clasped it with his own.

"Bitten off more than I can chew comes to mind,"
he said.

"Yes, but your sister has a chance now—and so
do the billions of people in the duchy," Helena said
as she squeezed his arm.

The Sword made the jump to Neres in seconds,
and they were now waiting for clearance down to
the navy yard landing base. More to do and more to
worry about ... he thought. Somehow, he knew
there would be more of those "can't fall asleep"

nights ahead too.

As she had ridden back to Neres City and the Barony Palace, she didn't think she would be this way. She was so angry she believed she'd be stomping the floors and breaking up furniture once she was in the private residential area of the palace.

Instead, she was coldly remote.

She had just missed out on the single best opportunity to gain new planets for the Barony, and she had been outsmarted by her son-in-law, Duke Scott.

While that infuriated her and she wondered what her blood pressure might have hit in the past few hours, she now was walking around her dead husband's old private study on the third floor of the residential part of the palace. She carried her wine but no glass; she swigged it directly from the bottle, ignoring how cold her hand was from holding the bottle of Quaran Pinot Grigio.

She had asked about the contents of the dressers and closets and even the big walk-in closet her stepdaughter used over in their part of the palace. In moments, she'd learned that they were empty. Helena and Tanner had surreptitiously moved all of their personal effects out of the palace. "Probably into the *Sword*, then to Juno, and now to Neen," she said to herself as she took another big swig of the white wine.

"Damn them—damn the dead duke as well!" she yelled. The Barony should have been the home for the billions of duchy citizens. That would have given her more planets than any other realm in the RIM Confederacy—and she would have become the new Council chairman.

That was her destiny, she knew.

Ambassador Bedre had no inkling that Tanner and Option Number Two were going to be exercised earlier today—that she was sure of.

The Caliph had even thought that his play of releasing the Tillion vid and blaming the event on the Duchy d'Avigdor, while faking the Barony signature on the production of the vid, would work. She knew better and she was sure that others at the Council table would as well. The fact that the whole Tillion issue—point number nine on the new business part of the Agenda just hours ago had been tabled for the next meeting was something else to think about for later.

But what had really surprised her was when she had glanced at the new Master Adept when the person to whom the duke had left the duchy to was named. She had known. She had known and she did not do anything about that, which she would have to think about more.

But now Tanner was not hers. He was the new Duke d'Avigdor, and that meant that he was an equal—no longer beneath her. He was a head of state. The duchy with its six-planet realm was only half the size of the Barony, but still it mattered.

He was now a worrisome competitor.

He knew about Ghayth.

He knew about the aliens—the Praix—and much of their secrets that he and his crew on the *Atlas* had found and been able to re-engineer for Barony use.

Behind that wall tapestry lay a door that went directly to the trophy room where someone had kept their kills from other worlds—worlds too far away to be able to be reached without cryonics. The Praix, she knew, were involved, but that was one secret she had not shared with anyone else.

There were many, many secrets within the Barony, and because of Tanner's marriage to Helena, he could now use those secrets, the ones he knew about, to his advantage.

He had friends all over the Barony Navy and even on the Hospital Ship, and she needed to think about that too. Perhaps I should purge the Barony of all of them? she thought. Send them all to ITO to be hard-rock miners for their remaining lives. Or just kill them. All of them, the new duke as well...

She swigged from the bottle again, and the

remains swished down her throat. She threw the empty bottle into the corner of the room where it smashed against a statue from God knew where.

"I will be the chairman," she said, "and it will be soon."

She barked at the study AI and demanded another bottle of the Pinot Grigio. "It better be here in seconds ..." she snarled.

Yes, she thought, maybe the best way to win was to simply rid the Confederacy of any threats to the Barony ...or in thinking more about it, maybe it might be time to find a way to use the new Duke....

Epilogue ~

He'd slept well, he thought, for at least the past few hours. Then, he'd slid off the bed and had been lost for a moment or two. It was his first night in the bedroom he and Helena had been asked to use this first night in the ducal palace. His palace concierge was a stickler, it seemed, for what was right and proper, so he'd begged the new duke to give him one day to make the real duke's bedroom chamber livable, as he'd called it, and Tanner had been so tired he readily accepted.

Helena had led him almost by the hand as they made their way up the three escalators within the public area of the duke's palace to the residential wing. They'd been put in one of the unused head of state bedrooms, which were held for use for visitors at any time.

She had been so much help, and the big press event of hours ago had gone well. Ambassador Bedre had introduced him as the new and rightful Duke d'Avigdor. Professor Bowen, the Confederacy constitutional expert had vetted him, and he'd had a turn at the microphone himself.

He'd welcomed the viewers and his new citizens to what he called a new day in the Duchy d'Avigdor, and he'd been as honest as he could have been. While he hadn't bothered pointing out

286

to the viewers that he was new to the position of being a duke, he felt that they knew that.

He'd been short and sweet in his first speech, but he had offered that he had an "open door" policy and that any citizen could be heard. Off camera, Ambassador Bedre had frowned when he said that, but that was too bad. Tanner wanted to know what his citizens wanted and what was important to them—just like he did when he'd been a navy captain in charge of his crew.

He padded over to the washroom thinking that at forty plus, perhaps he went to the john more than others. He shook his head as he peered at himself in the mirror. Gray at the temples, a pot on his lower stomach that looked like it might grow, and even, as he leaned in toward the mirror for a better look, a couple of gray chest hairs too.

"Wonder if the citizens need to know that," he said to himself as he grinned at his face in the mirror.

"Wonder what the citizens will want from me?" he said to himself as he padded back to the bed and slid in beside Helena, crabbing over to spoon her from behind.

He wrapped an arm over her waist. The new duke needed some downtime, he thought, and he slowly drifted back to sleep.

287

BOOK TWELVE OF THE RIM
CONFEDERACY

CAPTURED ALIENS

Prologue ~

The Praix had been in a hurry, suffering from
technology issues, yet they still made the seventy
nine thousand lights in less than an hour. At least
that was the first leg—and was to be followed by
more than a hundred more, as the ship tried to hide
it's real destination by using both inwards and

outwards milk-run locations in the Milkyway. It took more than four days to travel and double back and jump again and then back and then inwards and then outwards, as it hid it's real goal.

Copper plates at the back end of their huge craft almost glowed as they repelled away from the hastily jury-rigged satellite that they'd only a day ago. It had been handled by the Engineering Flock, and they swore that it would work. Not as quickly as the satellite that had been destroyed months ago on their home world—but it would get the Praix ship, the Wisp to it's destination.

As it came on it's path from it's own home behind it, lay waste and ruin.

As the central core cluster of the SagD galaxy, the Class III cluster had been more than the head of civilization for that small galaxy. It had taken more than fifty millennia for the Praix to rise from the branches of their home world trees to becoming the most powerful sentient race in SagD galaxy. They had settled on planets in the surrounding Local group of galaxies spread out over almost five million lights. There were now dozens of thousands of Praix colonies and here in SagD, they were being destroyed.

From where the invaders of SagD had come no one knew, not a single beak had been able to define where they had come from. But come they had.

These invaders did not communicate. They asked for nothing. They simply appeared in a system, eradicated any ships that they found. And moved on. And took nothing.

With more than ten thousand worlds in SagD being settled and colonies opening up still every year, the Praix had prided themselves on their ability to be a sane and civilized master race. Yes, there had been some small factions that had troubles being assimilated by the Praix, but with their superior technology, all had fallen before them. Some had been eradicated. Others offered slavery to remain alive at least. But all had fallen before the Praix.

Conquerors seldom face new forces that can withstand them—or defeat them.

And from what the Praix had seen, these invaders were simply eradicating anything they found. Everything they found.

So the appearance of this new unknown race with their smaller faster ships had been a surprise.

The Praix had fallen at each encounter. Their ships were destroyed by some kind of a beam sent out by these new invaders. Their planets had been simply burned up as the invaders dropped some kind of a bomb into their sun—and the resulting nova ended all life within the Cinderella zone.

The invaders moved like a black curtain across

SagD — destroying ships and putting out suns.

This was an invasion that had never been countenanced before...the death of an empire — at least in SagD.

So the Praix had fled.

Huge freighter ships were converted into refugee ships, carrying them away to other galaxies where safety might lie. From the large and small Magellanic clouds, Bootes, Ursa Major and Fornax and Andromeda too....all had been sent ships, tens of thousands of ships fled SagD.

There was no other way to look at it and this ship, the Wisp, had been well down the list when it came to safe-havens to run to. In fact, as there were few other locations, the Wisp had been sent into the huge Milkyway galaxy, to a location where the Praix had once considered for colonization in this galaxy — to Ghayth.

That experiment had gone awry, with the crash of the big freighter ship onto the planet itself, and the depositing of their slaves onto Eons. They'd not been back in twenty millennia — but the recent Ansible notation from Ghayth itself spoke of the ability of someone there, to let them once again, be the conqueror and not the conquered.

At least that's what the crew thought on the Wisp and they all perched, waiting to drop out of sub-space and into orbit around the planet...

Available in the fall of 2016!

Want to get early notice when we've got a new RIM Confederacy Series book launch?

Just drop by www.jimrudnick.ca and leave you email address and we'll let you know!

Or drop by our Face Book page at www.facebook.com/theRIMConfederacy/

Honeymoon Bottle

Dear Reader...

If you've made it this far, you're most likely thinking that this was the best SciFi you've ever read.

Or maybe not.

Maybe Tanner Scott wasn't your cup of tea?

Or you hate the Baroness and her scheming ways?

Or does the Caliph look like an upcoming tyrant?

So I'd like to ask you for a favor?

Would you mind taking a few minutes to write a review for me please?

And I'm talking honest too! Nothing makes us writers get better than book reviews!

Your comments help others know what to expect when they're looking for a great SciFi read...

And thanks once again, I'm looking forward to reading your comments!

Honeymoon Bottle

Jim Rudnick
2016